Mina, Etc

by LawrenceWilson

This book is dedicated to Jon Kettle
and to the boys and girls of the 2006-2007 Panthers Class
at Mayfield Primary School, East Sussex, UK,
who first heard the story told

Chapter One

I stood at the side of the stage, taking slow, deep breaths to calm myself—Mama suggested it when she dropped me off in front of the school. "I can't come in with you, Mina—I've three legal documents to go over with your Aunt Helena this morning, and your father needs to deliver those plans for the cathedral extension to your Uncle Lionel—but you'll be fine, promise. Just take a few deep breaths, and you'll be fine. You always are."

So slow, deep breaths it was. And Mama was right. I was fine. I am *always* fine. Well...*usually* fine. The things that seem to bother other kids my age—spiders, and unfamiliar food, and being left out of games—just don't seem to bother me. Not much, anyway. "Pluck," my great-aunt calls it. "My plucky girl!" Kind of an old-fashioned word, I guess, but she is an old-fashioned sort of lady.

But this—this was different. From the moment I'd walked through the forbidding iron gates into the grounds of Wallywood School, I'd felt—well, worried, somehow. Uncomfortable. Maybe it was just that I was wearing a neat, new Wallywood uniform in grey and dark blue wool plaid, which itched, rather. Maybe it was the way the heavy front door creaked, or the way the air smelled of dust, and boiled cabbage, and waxy furniture polish. Maybe it was just being back in England again, where the school system was so different, after being away so long. No matter—I was fine. I am *always* fine! That's what people expect, anyway. So—one deep breath, then another. A soft knock on the door to the school office, where an unsmiling, owlish-looking lady told me to go through to the hall, and pointed the way. My footsteps echoed on the black-and-red tiles in the empty, silent corridors.

So opening the door into the school hall was something of a shock. The din was incredible, like a flock of noisy, cheerful birds singing into microphones hooked up to powerful amplifiers. It was a vast, high-ceilinged room and very echoey, paneled with dark wood, and the tall pointed windows didn't actually seem to let in much light. The place was filled from front to back, from side to side, with children—tall, short, large, tiny, pretty, handsome, ordinary or silly-looking, brown-haired, black-haired, blond and ginger—all of them talking at once. I wanted to stick my fingers into my ears.

A short, round little man, whom I thought must be Mr Patel, the deputy headteacher (at my last school in the United States, we'd've called him an assistant principal), kept scurrying from side to side of the platform at the front of the hall, attempting to shush people.

"Attention, everyone!" he said over and over, waving his arms over his head, clapping his hands, and snapping his fingers. "Attention, please! Excuse me! Ahem, excuse me!"

No one paid him the slightest bit of attention.

Then Mrs Grimm, the headmistress, walked briskly into the room on her long, skinny, stork-like legs, smoothed her silver-streaked hair twice—quickly, once over each ear—and clapped her hands together softly, twice.

"Attention, everyone!" she said, barely raising her voice.

There was instant and complete silence. Scared silence. Rows and rows of silent, scared children in unattractive, itchy grey-and-blue-plaid uniforms...

Mrs Grimm smiled slightly, a very small, precise smile that barely stretched the corners of her mouth and certainly never reached her eyes. You have to watch out for teachers like that, the ones where the smile is only pasted on.

We all recited a prayer, and then a plump lady with spiky bleached-blonde hair and heavy black-lined eyes played a hymn on the piano, and we all sang. Mr Patel read some announcements which he said were very important, about littering and not running and queuing up properly in a neat queue while waiting to go in for lunch, but everyone ignored him. Then Mrs Grimm stood up to speak, and everyone immediately sat up straight and listened hard.

"As we begin the summer term, I'd like us all to welcome a new pupil to Wallywood School. Children, this is Mina Jones."

Deep breath! And I stepped out to join Mrs Grimm in the centre of the platform—me, Mina, neither tall nor short, large nor tiny, pretty nor plain. I'd just been with Mama to the hairdresser's for a trim, and my ordinary brown hair hung to my shoulders, cut into a fringe over my eyes. Nothing special about me, despite what my relatives all say, though I do think I have interesting pale blue eyes and I like my turned-up nose— okay, so perhaps I was a *little* scared, but I didn't act like it. I would *never* act like it, not in front of strangers. Instead, I simply looked out at the sea of children's faces and gave them a smile—and a real one, *not* a pasted-on one like Mrs Grimm's.

"Mina will be joining the Year 6s as of this morning. Amber, I'd like you to be Mina's special friend as she settles in. Would you do that for me?"

A tallish girl stood up towards the back of the hall. She had a friendly face with the craziest curly blonde-red-brown hair cut into a frizzy halo, and bright kiwi-fruit-green eyes, which really stood out against her café-au-lait-coloured skin. When she smiled, I could see the glitter of tooth braces.

"Of course, Mrs Grimm. I'd be glad to." Amber's voice had a bit of a rasp to it, as if she shouted a lot. Hmm…she could be one of those sporty types who want to play hockey and netball all the time. Why couldn't headteachers ever pick bookish kids to befriend new students? Amber walked jauntily up the aisle and bounded onto the platform to shake my hand, then walked to the door with me as the students milled about, exiting the hall.

4

"I'm Amber Anderson. Pleased to meet you."

"Mina. Mina Jones."

"Mina. That's a pretty name."

"Thank you," I said, and despite all those slow deep breaths, I bit my lip and let out just a little bit of a sigh. Only a tiny one! But Amber noticed, and pounced on it. She was a notice-er, was Amber.

"Are you all right? You look a little—upset."

I didn't really want to get into this discussion, but... "No, I'm fine, really. It's just that every time I start at a new school there's always trouble."

Amber's eyes went very round. "What sort of trouble?"

"It depends on the rules of the school."

A tall boy with dark hair and a smooth chocolate-brown complexion was hovering at Amber's elbow, and he laughed. "Oh, we have *lots* of rules here!"

Another boy, a short kid with freckles and spiky gingery hair, elbowed the tall one in the side. "Yeah, you'll always be in trouble at Wallywood if you don't watch out— unless you decide to play the teacher's pet, like Amber here!"

"That's not true, Zach Tolliver, and you know it! They're just trying to frighten you, Mina. Leave us alone, Zach! You, too, Joseph. Mrs Grimm didn't ask *you* to show Mina around today, did she?"

Joseph just grinned. "No, she didn't, but if the new girl is going to be in our class, we need to know something about her, don't we?"

"Yeah, c'mon, Mina," teased Zach. "Tell us everything! Like—why are you coming here two-thirds of the way through the year?"

"You don't have to answer them—" Amber started to say, pulling at my sleeve, but I always try to get along with everybody I meet, even boys.

"We just moved here," I told them. "We move around a lot because of my dad's work. He's an architectural engineer. We've just come back to England after a year in the United States."

The boys were silent for a little minute. Behind them, and behind Amber, I could see other kids hovering, listening. Well, why *wouldn't* they want to listen? If *I'd* been going to Wallywood since I was five years old, and one of *them* came along as a new kid, I'd be interested, too.

"America, huh?" said Zach, a wicked sort of gleam in his eye. "Where in America? Disney World?"

Disney World seems to be one of the few places in the United States that every British school-kid can identify. Doesn't anyone teach geography anymore? "No such luck," I told him. "Just a suburban kind of place in Illinois, near Chicago. My dad got to travel a lot, but my mum and I didn't, not so much."

"You don't really speak with an American accent, Mina," said Amber.

"My mum will be glad to hear that!" I laughed. "Every place we lived—Australia, South Africa, India, France, Russia, Romania—she's always nagging me to speak proper English."

"You've really lived all those places, Mina?" asked Amber, her eyes shining. "That's so exciting!"

"Exciting?" Moving every few months? Occasionally settling down for a whole year in one place, one house, one school? "It is, I guess." And I thought about the struggle to learn enough of a language to get by, just enough to purchase groceries and basically be polite to people. I remembered all the new schools I'd attended, some just for a month or two, and the good friends I'd made whom I'd had to leave behind when we moved again. "Yes, it is. But it doesn't always seem so exciting when you're doing it."

"You must be terrific in geography!" Amber giggled. "I'm sure not."

"No, you're only terrific at sucking up to the teachers…"

Other children started gathering around. Smiling faces, curious faces, one or two with a mean set to their mouths—you can always tell the bullies by the way they hold their mouths. I caught a few names—"I'm Jenny!" "I'm Abbie—this is my twin brother Andrew." "Welcome to Wallywood, Mina!"—but there was no sign of the teacher yet, and some of the boys started getting loud.

"You've got to watch out for Mrs Grimm, Mina," laughed one of the mean-mouthed boys—Ben, was it?—as he punched one of his mates. "She *loves* giving people detention!"

"People like *you*, Ben Simmons," snapped Amber. "Not people like Mina!"

"Oh, yeah? Come on, everybody, we need to tell the new girl what it's *really* like around here!"

"Ben! Give her that rap you wrote last term!" someone called out.

"But don't let the Grimm hear you," warned Zach, glancing down the corridor. "It almost got you suspended. You know, Mina, she's installed these miniature spy cameras everywhere, and can monitor every corner of the school without moving from her desk. They're even in the toilets."

"That's not true, Zach!" Amber insisted.

"Well, I wouldn't have put it past her…"

"I wish I had been suspended," Ben laughed. "I hate this place!" Then he started to chant, and some of the boys, and a few of the girls, joined in, clapping lightly to accompany him. It was obvious that they'd rehearsed it more than a few times!

ONLY *SPEAK* WHEN YOU'RE *SPOKEN* TO,

OR YOU'LL *END* UP IN THE *CORNER*
SITTING ON A *STOOL*.
PAY *ATTENTION* OR YOU RISK *DETENTION*—
THOSE ARE THE *RULES* THAT *RULE*
AT WALLYWOOD *SCHOOL*!

KEEP YOUR *HANDS* OUT OF YOUR *POCKETS*
WHEN YOU'RE *SPEAKING* TO THE *STAFF*.
ONLY SMILE WHEN A TEACHER SMILES—
YOU NEED WRITTEN *PERMISSION* TO *LAUGH*!

DID WE *MENTION*? BOYS STAND AT *ATTENTION*
AND *SALUTE* WHEN THE HEAD PASSES *BY*!
THE *GIRLS* ARE EXPECTED
TO *CURTSEY* INSTEAD
AND *NEVER* LOOK THE HEAD IN THE *EYE*!

DON'T TALK BACK!
DON'T PUT ON AIRS!
QUIET IN THE QUAD!
QUIET ON THE STAIRS!
SIT UP STRAIGHT!
DO AS YOU'RE TOLD!
NICE STRAIGHT LINES!
GEEZ, IT GETS OLD!

SO WATCH OUT, YOUR HIGHNESS,
OR YOU'RE SURE TO GET A MINUS—
THOSE ARE THE RULES THAT RULE
AT WALLYWOOD SCHOOL!

"Don't listen to them, Mina!" Amber hurried to reassure me. "It's really very nice here!"

"Thanks, Amber. I'm sure it is."

There was a sound behind us, a sharp sort of tap-tap-tapping, a pock-pock-pocking, a tick-tock-tick-tocking, which grew steadily in volume. I knew that sound—any kid would! It was the same sound you hear in any school, anywhere: high-heeled shoes on floor tiles, getting nearer....

"Watch it, guys! Here comes the Grimm!"

Mrs Grimm appeared from around the corner, followed by Mr Patel and a harried-looking woman with black hair and black-rimmed glasses who must be my new teacher. "A little less noise, Year 6. Line up properly, please. Miss Marquardt, would you take your class inside? Not you, Mina," she said, as I started to get into line behind Amber. "If you'd come with me, please. We need a little more information for our school records."

"A little more information," Mr Patel echoed, but Mrs Grimm ignored him, as did Miss Marquardt, and as did all of Year 6. He glanced from side to side, blinking forlornly, as the corridor emptied.

Poor man. I flashed him a quick grin as I turned to follow Mrs Grimm, and was rewarded with a startled blink of his sad brown eyes, followed by the brightest, most surprised and delighted smile I'd ever seen.

"Mina! This way, please," snapped Mrs Grimm. "And Amber, you might come along so that you can take Mina back to the classroom. This will just take a few minutes."

Amber nodded with a mumbled "Yes, ma'am," then she and Mr Patel and I obediently followed Mrs Grimm towards that dreaded chamber of secrets and horrors—the Headteacher's Office….

CHAPTER 2

Mrs Grimm sat herself behind her desk in her high-backed chair, opened a fat manila file folder and raised her reading glasses from their chain around her neck. "Let's start right at the beginning, shall we?"

"At the beginning," Mr Patel agreed, settling himself into one of the visitor's chairs across from her. I took the other one, and Amber sat in a chair by the open door. I glanced this way and that from the corners of my eyes—nope, no handcuffs, no manacles, no torture devices—just an ordinary office with yellow-painted walls, a vast wooden desk and a row of metal filing cabinets opposite the tall narrow window. There was a pretty bouquet of roses in a blue vase next to Mrs Grimm's computer, but when I looked closely I could see that they were artificial. Rather like her smile….

"Now—Is 'Mina' your full name, dear?"

I knew it. I knew it! Trouble, first thing, just as I'd told Amber there would be.

"My full name?" I asked slowly.

"Yes, dear. 'Mina.' Is it your full name, or a nickname?"

"A nickname?"

Mrs Grimm let out a brief sigh. I knew that sort of sigh. You don't pass through as many schools as I have and not recognise it. *Trouble!* I hadn't been in Wallywood for half an hour yet and I was already annoying the headteacher.

"What I mean, of course, my dear, is Mina short for something?"

(I really hate being called "my dear" by people who don't think I'm actually dear to them…)

"Short for something?"

Mr Patel let out a little snort of what could have been amusement. "Does she have to repeat everything you say?"

Mrs Grimm glared at him over her glasses. "I'm sure she's just a little nervous, Clive. It is her first day and all… What I'm asking, dear, is what is 'Mina' short for? I need your full name for my official form."

(I knew this was going to happen!)

"My *full* name? Well…I was named after my Great-Aunt Wilhemina…"

"Now, that's a *lovely* name! Let me write that down… Not one you hear so much nowadays, I must say… I have an Aunt Wilhemina myself, you know."

"Do you really, ma'am? Maybe we're related!"

Mr Patel snorted again, and Mrs Grimm permitted her lips to stretch into what I am sure she thought was a tolerant smile. "I hardly think so, dear. There. 'Wilhemina.' I think we shall continue to call you 'Mina,' if that's all right? Except on official reports and such… Now, do you have a middle name?"

(Trouble!) "A middle name?"

"She's doing it again," muttered Mr Patel.

Mrs Grimm paused, holding the pen in her long, well-manicured fingers like a miniature orchestra conductor's baton, and then spoke slowly and over-exaggeratingly-clearly, as if I were a five-year-old just beginning Year 1. "Do you have a *second* name, Mina?"

"A *second* name? Oh, yes! I have a *second* name. It's Frederika."

"How very elegant!" said Mrs Grimm with that same false smile. "F-R-E-D-E-R-I...?"

"K-A. I was named after my Great-Uncle Frederik, the Grand Duke of Haunau-Brauncau."

There was a distinct pause. Mrs Grimm's eyes had gone rather wide behind her glasses, and Mr Patel's mouth had dropped open a half-inch.

Amber leaned close and whispered, "Really, Mina? You really have an uncle who's a Grand Duke?"

"Oh, yes! My great-uncle. Actually my great-*great*-uncle. Haunau-Brauncau isn't a very *big* country, of course. It's high up in the mountains, and very pretty. We go skiing there in the winter."

Mrs Grimm had recovered her composure. "Well, Mina, that's very—I mean, how wonderful to have—I mean, let me just write that down. "Wilhemina Frederika—"

"Alexandra," I added quickly.

14

There was another distinct pause. (Not really the sort of distinct pause that you want to hear when sitting on a hard chair in the headteacher's office...)

"I beg your pardon?" asked Mrs Grimm.

I took a deep breath. "I said, 'Alexandra,' ma'am. It's the next bit of my name. After my mother's cousin, Alexandra Lyps-Hyanova."

Mrs Grimm blinked. "Alexandra Lyps-Hyanova? The ballet dancer?"

Amber's green eyes had gone very wide indeed.

Mr Patel grunted. "Who?"

Mrs Grimm's lips pursed into a prim, superior little moue. "Only the prima ballerina at the Imperial Malakhov Ballet of St Petersburg, Clive! Only one of the most famous dancers in the world!"

"Oh. Her. Of *course*. Her. Sorry. Silly of me."

"She's *totally* my idol!" whispered Amber. "She's *amazing!*"

"Well, everyone says so," I whispered back. "Last year when we saw her dance in Rome, she took twelve curtain calls, and everyone kept throwing flowers onto the stage!"

"Oh, dear, I am running out of room..." murmured Mrs Grimm. "Maybe if I squeeze it in sideways... Well, Mina, that is certainly *most* interesting. Perhaps your cousin might agree to come to Wallywood to give a talk to some of our girls..."

15

"I'm sure she would, ma'am. I believe she's dancing in London this December, and she always sends us tickets. Antoinette," I added.

Now Mrs Grimm's eyes narrowed. (I know that look, and you know it, too—it means that the grown-up to whom you're talking thinks you're not exactly telling the truth…) "Oh, dear, Mina. *Another* name? What relative is it *this* time?"

"Another cousin, ma'am. My cousin Antoine. Antoine LaVitesse. The race car driver."

Mrs Grimm looked completely blank, as did Amber, but Mr Patel sat right up and his face lit up like a little boy's. "Antoine LaVitesse! He's won the Grand Prix seven times!"

"Eight," I corrected him. "Yes, he and my mother are very close. We stay with him whenever we go to the south of France."

"Well, I must say! That is quite exciting," Mrs Grimm admitted, scribbling away on her form. "What very interesting family get-togethers you must have! Perhaps you could invite your cousin to visit Wallywood to give a little talk at assembly. I'm sure that the boys would be most interested…"

"Yes, they would!" interrupted Mr Patel loudly. Mrs Grimm glowered at him. "Sorry, Hester."

"I'd be happy to ask him, ma'am," I said, as her pen scratched on the paper. Then: "Persimmon."

Mrs Grimm laid her pen down with a sharp clatter. "Not another name!"

16

"Yes, ma'am. Sorry, ma'am. I was named after my aunt, the writer."

Mrs Grimm's mouth dropped open, and then she slowly rose from her seat, two bright spots of pink glowing on her cheeks. (Trouble! Oh, trouble indeed…)

"Mina, you are *not* sitting there and telling me that you are related to Persimmon Jones?"

I gulped. "Yes, ma'am, I am. She's one of my father's older sisters. Why, have you read her books?"

"Read them? Read them?" Mrs Grimm glanced away from me, over my head, out the door, and her eyes went suddenly soft and unfocused, as if she were looking at something wonderful located somewhere very far away… "Of course I've read them! Persimmon Jones is my favourite author in the entire world! *Sweet and Sour Surrender… The Passion and the Plum… The Lost Rose of Timbuktu…*"

Amber, alert as always, leaned over to me. "Are her books really that good?" she whispered.

"I don't really know," I whispered back. "My mother won't let me read them until I'm eighteen."

Mrs Grimm came back to earth with a shiver and a shake of her narrow shoulders. "Well, I certainly have to find room somewhere on my form for *that* name…"

I breathed a sigh of relief. "Thank you, ma'am. I know she'd appreciate it. And try to make room for 'Sylvia,' too.

"Sylvia?" Mrs Grimm frowned at me as if I were speaking Swahili. "Sylvia? Whatever for?"

"Because I know that Auntie Persimmon would be very upset if her twin sister's name were left off your form. Sylvia—S-Y-L-V-I-A. Sylvia Golduste. The actress."

There was another one of those pauses. But this one went on and on…

"The movie actress?" I ventured. "You might have heard of her…?"

Mrs Grimm stared.

Mr Patel stared.

Amber stared.

Not one of them spoke.

"Of course, it's not her REAL name," I added hurriedly, trying to fill that dangerous silence. "But her agent thought that 'Prudence Jones' wouldn't look very nice on the marquee… So she changed it."

Not a word from Mrs Grimm. Not a grunt from Mr Patel. Not a whisper from Amber. Oh, dear…

Finally Mrs Grimm's cheek twitched. "A movie star!" she breathed.

"A movie star!" gasped Mr Patel.

"A real movie star!" sighed Amber, so softly that I could barely hear her.

"Yes, ma'am. Yes, sir."

Suddenly Mrs Grimm's eyes began to narrow, and a deep line appeared between her eyebrows.

I tried to avert disaster: "They both live in Paris, but I'm sure they wouldn't mind visiting the school the next time they're in England! They love signing autographs!"

Mrs Grimm cleared her throat. Then she cleared it again.

"Ahem…ahem!…Wilhemina…Frederika…Alexandra …Antoinette…Persimmon…Sylvia…This is getting a wee bit ridiculous, Mina."

I hung my head. "I'm very sorry to hear you say that, ma'am…"

"I should hope so!"

"…because there's one more. Constantinople."

Mrs Grimm was shaking her head. "No, Mina. *No*, Mina. No, Mina. Not possible, Mina. I mean, look at my form, there just isn't *room*. I can't possibly— Really, Mina, I must insist— Er, did you say 'Constantinople?'"

"Yes, ma'am, I did."

"Constantinople Jones? The celebrity chef?

"Yes, ma'am. He's my uncle," I said, then added quickly, as Mrs Grimm opened her mouth for what I was certain would be a roar, "and I'm sure he'd love to come and give a cooking demonstration!"

Mrs Grimm slowly placed her pen in its holder and, even more slowly, leaned back in her chair. "Mina," she said, her voice dropping low and soft, pretending to be sympathetic and concerned—do grown-ups really think that kids can't tell when they're faking? "These famous relatives of yours. So many of them... Are you telling us the truth?"

My spine straightened. My head came up. My chin lifted. I looked her straight in the eyes. "I never lie, Mrs Grimm," I said, and heard my own voice go all cold and formal, sounding just like Auntie Sylvia's in her last movie, in that scene where the nasty mean-mouthed barrister was accusing her of perjury in the witness stand...

I don't know what expression was on my face, but apparently Mrs Grimm didn't care for it very much. She leaned across her desk blotter, her mouth set in a tight horizontal line and the blotches on her cheeks redder than ever. "It's too *much*, Miss Jones! It's *too* much! Look at this form! I mean, *look* at this *form*! This is an *official* form, Mina! And it's a *mess*!"

"I know, ma'am," I said calmly as I could. "And I'm sorry, ma'am. But you did say that you wanted my full name."

"How many names does she have?" muttered Mr Patel. "I've lost count."

Amber started ticking them off on her fingers. "Seven, I think, sir."

"I don't care if it's seven or seventeen, Amber! It's too *many*! *That's* how many it is! *Too* many!" Mrs Grimm waved one hand at the paper in front of her as if by doing so she could

20

rub out all the scribbles and crossings-out and tiny, crabbed letters—and rub me out of her school, as well. She sat down abruptly and glared at the paper through her spectacles. "Wilhemina Frederika Alexandra Antoinette Persimmon Sylvia Constantinople *Jones*," she read aloud in a sarcastic voice. "Too many! *Too many!*" Steepling her fingers together, her eyes narrowed. "What *could* your parents have been thinking?"

I bit my lip—I was *not* going to cry in front of this horrible beaky bird of a woman! "When I was born, ma'am, my parents didn't want to offend any of their relatives, and—and—Please! Couldn't you just write down 'Mina, Etc,' ma'am? That's what my last school did."

"What a ridiculous suggestion, Mina! This is an *official form*! It needs an *official name*! 'Mina, Etc,' indeed!" She stood, towering over me and looking more like a stork than ever. "Now, you are going to go to your classroom and I am going to speak to your parents, and then you and your parents may speak to all those ridiculous relatives of yours and in—in a week, one week, I expect you to have chosen one single name. One! Do you understand me? *One* week! *One* name! Amber, take her—away! *Away!* You stay, Clive! I want you to hear this." And Mr Patel, who'd half-risen to flee the fury of the Grimm, sat down again. He gave me a weak little smile as Amber and I slid out the half-opened door.

21

The school secretary was staring, her mouth a perfect O (oh, trouble indeed! You never want to mess with the school secretary! They know *everybody's* secrets). Amber kept tugging at my arm, but I resisted, and we both stood there, in the corridor just outside the office, for a long minute, listening to the headteacher's ferocity spewing down the telephone lines in a shrill torrent of angry words.

I sighed.

"Are you okay, Mina?" Amber whispered.

"Yes, thanks."

"She didn't have to tell you off like that."

"No...but this always happens..."

"Still, it wasn't very nice of her to call your relatives 'ridiculous.' What are you going to do?"

My mother, ever the peacemaker, would hurriedly agree with everything Mrs Grimm was saying, but... I sighed again. Mrs Grimm had no idea what my relatives were like. "Strong-minded" doesn't really cover it... Try "selfish," bossy," "impractical" or even "determined-to-have-their own-way-at-all-times." Our family reunions were more than "interesting"—they usually descended into something closely resembling hand-to-hand combat...

"Which name do you think you'll choose, Mina? One name out of seven—wow, that'll be tough."

One name? I had to choose just one name? Impossible. My aunts and uncles and cousins wouldn't give up without a fight....

"If I know my relatives," I told Amber, "they'll want to discuss this in person. I may have to do some quick traveling...Germany and Russia and Paris and Monaco...."

Amber's eyes lit up. "How exciting! All those wonderful places! You're really lucky, Mina." She pushed open the door to the Year 6 room, where Miss Marquardt was vainly trying to quiet the class for a maths lesson.

"Lucky? I guess so... It's just that..."

Then Amber boomed out in her big sporty voice, "Hey, guys, you'll never guess what happened in Mrs Grimm's office!" And I had to tell the whole thing all over again to everyone in Year 6.

I have to say, there are some really nice kids at Wallywood School. Even the bullies, with their thin, nasty little mouths, seemed—I don't know, sort of nice. Supportive, anyway. Willing to be friends. Maybe because Amber and Zach and Joseph seemed to want to be friends. Or maybe just because I had an interesting story to tell...

We never did get to the maths lesson. So maybe I am lucky. I hate maths.

CHAPTER 3

That evening, Daddy arranged for a special conference line so that everyone could talk at the same time. Big mistake, in my opinion! It sounded like feeding time in the tiger cage at the zoo, electronically enhanced by modern technology.

Great-Uncle Frederik bellowing at Daddy. Cousin Alexandra simpering at Mama. Cousin Antoine acting cool and calm and collected, but practically spitting with belligerence. Auntie Persimmon and Auntie Sylvia in a sort of mirror-image rage—they can't bear each other, but they sound almost exactly alike and scream with almost exactly the same degree of posh theatricality. Uncle Constantinople threatening—I could almost see him, stomping around his vast fancy kitchen, waving his big butcher's knife ominously...Their usual selves, their usual larger-than-life personalities, their usual booming voices clamouring for your attention. It was "Me, first! Me, first! Me! Me! ME!" with them, every time, all the time...

Only Great-Aunt Wilhemina kept her voice low and soothing, but even she was firm with my parents that a prompt visit was in order. "And I know you're both incredibly busy just now, but you mustn't worry about her traveling alone, my dears," she reassured my mum. "She's done it before—our plucky little girl!"

Mama was practically in tears, and Daddy definitely looked singed around the edges. But when the relatives spoke to me, their voices were practically cooing.

COME FOR A VISIT, DARL-ING!
COME FOR A VISIT, DEAR-IE!
COME AND STAY, JUST A BRIEF HOLIDAY
AWAY FROM THAT SCHOOL SO DREAR-Y

YOU'VE GOT A BIG DECISION
I CAN HELP YOU TO MAKE...
CHOOSE *MY* NAME!
CHOOSE *MINE*!
CHOOSE *MINE*!
CHOOSE *MINE*!
YOU DON'T WANT TO MAKE A MISTAKE!

COME FOR A VISIT, DEAR-IE!
YOU NEED A LITTLE REST
CAN'T TAKE ANY MORE
OF THESE CHOICES GALORE?
YOU HAVE TO DECIDE WHAT'S BEST.
COME FOR A VISIT, LOVE-Y!
JUST FOR A DAY OR TWO
TO SETTLE THIS BUSINESS OF WHAT
SINGULAR NAME TO CHOOSE...

CHOOSE *MINE*!

CHOOSE *MINE*!

CHOOSE *MINE*!

"I will see her tomorrow," barked Great-Uncle Frederik. "Haunau-Braunkau is the logical place to start."

"Paris is closer," snarled Auntie Persimmon and Auntie Sylvia simultaneously.

"I shall await her in St Petersburg on Wednesday," purred Cousin Alexandra. "I shall send the Imperial Malakhof Ballet's private jet."

"Selfish of you, Lexie," spat Cousin Antoine. "It's a long way from Russia to the south of France... but I'll pick her up Thursday morning at the airport in Nice. I have a little treat in store for her that day..."

"As have I, of course," murmured Cousin Alexandra.

"It will be a most glorious visit!" roared Great-Uncle Frederik.

"Well, I want her in Paris by one o'clock on Friday at the LATEST," snapped Auntie Persimmon. "The fast train leaves Nice at 7:15 am."

Aunt Sylvia spoke at the same time, in her rich, resonant voice that could reach the back row of any theatre. "Put her on the TGV at 7:15, Antoine. She *needs* to be in Paris by one o'clock."

26

"BBC studios in London, first thing on Saturday afternoon," growled Uncle Constantinople. "That's when— we'll never mind, just make sure she's there."

"If you'd like, Mina, dear," said Great-Aunt Wilhemina softly, "you could spend Saturday night with me. I'll fix us a nice little supper and we can have a talk, and I can send you back to your parents on Sunday morning. How does that sound, dear?"

"Perfect, Aunt Wilhemina," I said, then added hurriedly, before the tide of indignation could rise and drown us all with further shouting, "I mean, it all sounds perfect. I am so looking forward to seeing all of you."

Remember how I told Mrs Grimm that I never lie? That wasn't exactly the truth. Oh, I can be such a good little fibber when I need to be! You wouldn't think it, to look at me, would you? Butter wouldn't melt in my mouth, as the old saying goes. I would never lie in order to cheat somebody or take advantage, but...but can you honestly say that lying is such a bad thing, really, when you do it to keep peace amongst your relatives? Your selfish, *loud* relatives?

When everything was arranged and everyone had rung off and the echoes of all their yelled demands and accusations and had finally faded away, Daddy went out for takeaway pizza, because we hadn't unpacked all the dishes and silverware yet, and we weren't sure where the removal men had put the rest of the dining room chairs. It's always like that, the first couple of days after we move. Lots of meals eaten standing up, or with a plate balanced on your knees while you perched on a packing crate. Mama lay down for a few minutes with a cold compress over her eyes—we *had* found the beds and the sheets and blankets and pillows, at least—and I telephoned Amber and told her everything.

I also mentioned that I'd been a bit surprised at how—well, *interested* the rest of the class had been when I told them about my relatives.

"Well, what do you expect, Mina?" Amber asked in a practical tone of voice. "An uncle who's a duke, and that race-car driver—you should have heard Zach Tolliver at home time, going on about the Grand Prix while we waiting by the school gates! And everyone watches *Constantinople's Kitchen* on the telly on Saturdays—everyone!"

"I know, I know, but—"

"Is he really your uncle? Oh, I know he is, you said he is, but—well, he's mixed-race, isn't he? Like me? I mean, his skin is pretty dark."

"He's my dad's half-brother. My grandfather married Grandma Connie after his first wife, my Granny Louisa, died. But it sounds stupid to call him my half-uncle..."

"Yeah, you're right, it does. And once someone is family, then they're family, that's what my mum says. She insists that I have to call all my older cousins 'auntie,' and it gets pretty confusing sometimes."

"Oh, yes, it does!"

"But your relatives—wow! I mean, one of Joseph's uncles is pretty rich—he works in the City and he's always giving Joseph new bicycles and electronic games and all these other really fancy presents—and I have an aunt who owns this speciality Jamaican sweet shop, which is great if you like sugar and chocolate and tropical fruit, but it's certainly can't compare to your family." Amber sounded positively wistful.

"It's—it's not as agreeable as it sounds, Amber, really. They're all so used to getting their own way that other people just get sort of steamrolled under... I just know that each of them is going to try to make me choose *his* name or *her* name and none of them are going to expect any arguments! Except my Great-Aunt Wilhemina. You'd like her—she's really sweet and kind. Smart and funny, too. But she's the only one!"

"Hmm," mused Amber. "I can see how it's going to be difficult. But I think that you should choose the name you like best, Mina. It's you who has to live with it. Sure, you have to go visit them, but it has to be your decision, right?"

"Right..."

"Right. You've got a good head on your shoulders, Mina. You go visit everyone, and then come back and tell Mrs Grimm what you've decided. It'll be okay, you'll see. And maybe you could send us some postcards from all those wonderful places...?"

29

"Sure, I can do that. First stop—my Great-Uncle Frederik's castle!"

I heard Amber gasp on the other end of the line. "An uncle who lives in a real genuine castle? See, you really *are* a lucky girl, Mina!"

"Listen, I have to ring off—my dad is back with the pizza."

"And I have to set the table and finish my homework before dinner. Lucky you! One day of school and then you're on holiday for a week!"

"Well, not *exactly* a holiday… and there are all kinds of luck, Amber. Wish me some! I'm going to need it."

CHAPTER 4

"Mina!" bellowed Great-Uncle Frederik from the top of the stone steps, with the enormous stone castle rising behind him, grey as a petrified storm-cloud, overcrowded with turrets and flagpoles and balconies and pointed windows. "My very favourite grand-niece in the whole entire world! Welcome! Welcome! A thousand times welcome to Haunau-Brauncau!"

"Thank you, Uncle Frederik," I said, dropping the most formal curtsey I could manage and trying to stifle a yawn. Mama and Daddy had put me on a very early flight to Munich, where Great-Uncle Frederik's enormous vintage chauffeur-driven Daimler limousine had been waiting to whisk me into the depths of the Bavarian Alps. It truly is a beautiful part of the world—gorgeous mountains, thick green forests threaded with waterfalls, tidy little farms and pastures filled with the honey-coloured cows which provided the rich, creamy milk that they use to make the famous Haunau-Brauncau cheeses. But I was a bit too groggy to appreciate it. I hadn't slept especially well the night before, as my mind keep churning and circling, over and over, circling and churning, which name to choose, which name to choose...

"Welcome!" Great-Uncle Frederik bawled again, louder than ever, his face redder than ever, his huge mustache (bigger than ever) bristling as he smiled. Weird... Why was he dressed in his fur-trimmed robe of state, which barely met around his fatter-than-ever round belly? And why was he wearing the ducal coronet and a chestful of medals? Why were so many colourful banners flying? And why were all the castle's servants lined up along the sides of the staircase, in their severe black and white uniforms, like something out of a scene in one of Auntie Sylvia's movies?

Why were so many people gathered in the town square, dressed in their colourful old-fashioned festival clothes? I mean, no one wears lederhosen and hats with badges and feathers and dirndl dresses and embroidered blouses and shawls anymore, not for everyday. Obviously, Great-Uncle Frederik must be trying to make an impression of some sort. There was even a brass band assembled to one side, made up of a dozen men in bright red uniforms. Why had my uncle decided that we needed music?

"Welcome, Mina," Great-Uncle Frederik roared, glaring at everyone assembled.

"Welcome, Mina," the people echoed obediently—and unenthusiastically.

"Hello, Uncle. Hello, everyone. Thank you for inviting me. It's lovely to be here again." My German was pretty rusty, but I'd practised a bit on the flight and I'm sure that I said that correctly. Well, fairly correctly.

"Well, we must be very sure that you make the right decision about your name, eh? Eh? Of course we must! Ha-ha-ha!"

"Ha-ha-ha," laughed the servants, right on cue.

"Ha-ha-ha," laughed the gathered townsfolk, a little less certainly.

"And to be very sure, very sure indeed, I have prepared a very special treat for my very special niece, eh?" One of the musicians stood up and set his trumpet to his lips, letting loose a long squeaky note like a strangling goose. Great-Uncle Frederik reached inside his coat and pulled out something golden and shiny, glittering with gemstones. It was a miniature version of the coronet he wore himself. Beaming with pride, he settled it onto my head—where it fit perfectly. The servants in their two neat rows applauded politely, echoed by the people standing in the square.

"Oh, my goodness—Uncle Frederik, thank you! It's beautiful!"

He leaned in close and gave me a big sloppy kiss on the ear. His mustache tickled. "It was my own dear sister's when she was a young girl. Your great-grandmother's, you see? So it is only right that you wear it now, when you—" and he paused dramatically before bellowing out—"when you rule the Grand Duchy of Haunau-Brauncau for one whole day!"

"Huzzah," came the polite, if lukewarm, response from the gathered Haunau-Brauncauvians.

"But—oh, but, Uncle—thank you, but I don't know anything about ruling a Duchy!"

33

"Pshaw! There is nothing to it! Being a Grand Duke is the easiest thing in the world! Whatever you say, *that* is the law! My people never give me any trouble! And if they do— well, that's what dungeons are for, right? Of course, right! Ha- ha-ha!" The orchestra began a squeaky seesaw kind of music, sounding rather like a complaining donkey, and Great-Uncle Frederik turned to face the people gathered in the square in front of the castle, opened his big mouth and began to sing:

I'M THE GENTLEST OF RULERS!
I'M THE KINDEST OF ALL MEN!
I TAKE CARE OF ALL MY SUBJECTS
LIKE A SWEET OLD MOTHER HEN!
NO ONE EVER GIVES ME TROUBLE
SUCH GOOD MANNERS THEY REMEMBER
BECAUSE THEY KNOW
THEY WOULDN'T LIKE IT
IF I HAD TO LOSE MY TEMPER!

THERE'S A WRONG WAY AND A RIGHT WAY
TO RULE A LAND LIKE THIS
AND WHAT I PREFER IS *MY* WAY—
THAT'S TO POUND AN IRON FIST!
DON'T YOU DARE TO GIVE ME BACK-TALK!
DON'T YOU DARE TO TELL ME "NO!"

BECAUSE YOU KNOW YOU WOULDN'T LIKE IT
IN MY DUNGEONS FAR BELOW!

There was a clip-clop of horses' hooves, and from around the corner trotted two grey horses, with bright ribbons braided in their manes, pulling a fancy little open-topped carriage which was painted glossy jet-black with gold trimming and red leather seats. A footman sprung forward to open the door, and Great-Uncle Frederik, with a huge smile on his round face, handed me up into the carriage seat himself. He then huffed and puffed himself into the seat beside me, settling with an "oof" of expelled breath. The carriage sagged a bit on the side he was sitting. I felt sorry for the horses that had to pull us.

The carriage driver clucked at the horses, and we set off across the square and down the main street of the town. The Haunau-Brauncauvians, in their colourful costumes, waved and smiled. Great-Uncle Frederik waved and beamed, beamed and waved, and went on singing:

I'M THE NICEST DUKE IN EUROPE!
DON'T YOU THINK MY ROBES ARE FINE?
PEOPLE NEVER GIVE YOU PROBLEMS
WHEN YOU RULE BY RIGHT DIVINE!
SO I BUILD ANOTHER CASTLE!
SO I BUY ANOTHER CROWN!

35

JUST KEEP WAVING AND KEEP SMILING
WHEN I DEIGN TO RIDE THROUGH TOWN!

We turned a corner—a bit difficult, on those narrow medieval streets—and, seemingly out of nowhere, people popped out of doorways and alleyways and leaned out windows to wave and smile.

THERE'S A WRONG WAY AND A RIGHT WAY
TO RULE A LAND LIKE THIS
AND WHAT I PREFER IS *MY* WAY—
THAT'S TO POUND AN IRON FIST!
WE'VE A LONG AND GLORIOUS HISTORY
FIRST IN WAR AND FIRST IN PEACE
SO IT'S REALLY QUITE A MYSTERY
WHY WE'RE ONLY KNOWN FOR CHEESE…

As we negotiated another narrow corner (and more people popped out of doorways and windows to wave at us), I found myself staring at Great-Uncle Frederik with my mouth hanging open. I mean, I know that I'd heard Daddy refer to him as a "tin-plated old despot"—and I had had to look up that last word, which I'd never heard before (it means a sort of tyrant, or an absolutely ruler of a country, someone with whom you're not allowed to argue, not ever). Now, I know that Haunau-Braunkau isn't a very big country, or officially even a

36

country at all, but you would think that Great-Uncle Frederik wouldn't really have the right, in this modern day and age, I mean, to pound his fist and throw someone into a dungeon, just for disagreeing with him...would he? Or that he'd spend money on castles and crowns when it was obvious that Haunau-Braucau could use a bit of modernisation when it came to things like pavements and road-signs and streetlamps...

The inside bits of the elaborate gold trimmings on the carriage were rather dusty. The leather cushions were starting to split and the stuffing was coming out. And as we turned another tight corner, and more townsfolk waved, I was sure that I'd just seen that one particular blonde-haired girl in the red dirndl a minute ago, waving the exact same flag—and that boy with the cheeky grin in the embroidered lederhosen and the feather in his cap... And that man with the curly moustache... and that lady with the basket of paper flowers....

Then we were back at the main square in front of the castle, surrounded by a cheering (and panting) crowd, whom I swear had just ducked through those narrow twisty back lanes to beat us there... There was a photographer from the *Münchner Merkur* whose camera kept flashing and flashing as he darted about looking for the best shot.

"So, Mina," Great-Uncle Frederik began in a loud voice which carried to all corners of the square, "now that you are wearing the crown—Hey, you!" he bellowed, pointing abruptly at someone in the front row. "And you! And you and you and you! Bow to my niece, eh? Bow! That's better—So, Mina, what are your orders?"

I must have looked as befuddled and confused as one of the Duchy's famous cows when faced with an unfamiliar weed in her favourite patch of grass. "My orders?"

"As Grand Duchess of Haunau-Brauncau—temporary Grand Duchess, that is—your loyal subjects await your commands! Don't you?" he snarled genially at the townsfolk and servants, who all agreed instantly that they did, sir, they did, Your Grace, they did, of course—all of them looking at Great-Uncle Frederik with a strange sort of look on their faces. The sort of look I'd seen kids back at Wallywood giving Mr Patel—and I was suddenly certain that Great-Uncle Frederik would have preferred that his subjects looked at him the way the kids looked at Mrs Grimm....

And the way that all the gathered people were looking at me...Summing me up. Wondering if I were like my uncle... Oh, I didn't like that at *all*!

"So go ahead! Everyone is waiting. They will all do *exactly* as you say. *Won't you?*"

And again that sort-of-half-frightened hubbub of agreement—of course, Your Grace, anything you say, Your Grace. They were smiling, every last person standing below me and lined up alongside of me, but Great-Uncle Frederik must have ordered those smiles, because they were false. Fake! Completely fake. I could tell. Anyone could tell.

Did my uncle really think that you could command someone to be happy?

And then I smiled.

"Um...I declare a holiday!"

The people in the crowd glanced at each other as if they were uncertain what the word meant.

"A holiday!" beamed Great-Uncle Frederik loudly. "What a wonderful idea! You see how my grand-niece thinks about the welfare of the people of Haunau-Brauncau? You will all cheer now."

And the crowd obediently cheered. Not especially enthusiastically. It was like the noise that you might make when you find your second-to-least favourite pudding on the lunch menu. I mean—could be worse. Could be stewed prunes, right?...but... "Hooray." The photographer's camera flashed.

Great-Uncle Frederik smiled right and left, waving his plump hand as if their cheering had actually meant something. "Good, good... and what else?"

What else? "Uh... All the schools will be closed! And...um...there will be dancing in the streets!"

The cheering was a bit more enthusiastic this time, especially from the school-aged children whom I could see. They were all grinning broadly.

39

"Oh, I like what I am hearing!" Great-Uncle Frederik shouted jovially. "What a fine Grand Duchess you will make someday...What else?"

"Um...All the prisoners will be released from the dungeons!"

"Fine, fine—eh, what was that?"

There were three full seconds of stunned silence before genuine, heartfelt, happy laughter erupted from the crowd.

"There's nothing in those dungeons but cheese!" someone called out. I thought it might have been the boy with the cheeky grin. "Hasn't been for years!"

"He's just pretending!" shouted the girl in the red dirndl. "He likes to pretend!"

Great-Uncle Frederik's eyes were narrowing, and his eyebrows bunching together like worried caterpillars. "My dear great-niece," he muttered out of the side of his mouth, while continuing to smile and wave at the people, "I do not believe that you quite understand the seriousness of what you are saying."

"Oh, I understand it perfectly, Uncle," I answered just as softly, before raising my voice to its loudest: "And everyone in Haunau-Braunkau will receive five—no, *seven* gold pieces!"

The roar of their astonished delight was probably heard back in Munich.

"What? What?" Great-Uncle Fredrik was shouting. "Do you want to bankrupt me?"

"But Uncle, you *said*—"

"I know what I said! But you—"

"You said that whatever I said would be the law, just as it is when *you* say it."

"Of course I said that, you silly little girl, but I never meant—"

I *knew* he hadn't. "So you don't *really* want me to rule Haunau-Brauncau for a day, do you, Uncle Frederik? So all this—the music and the costumes and great-grandmother's coronet—is really just some silly bribe, to get me to choose your name, isn't it?"

"Of course it isn't—" Great-Uncle Frederik began to sputter. "Of course I want you to—Of course…I mean…That is…I…I…I…."

"And there aren't actually that many people left in town, are there, Uncle? It's been the same three or four dozen people cheering us from the minute we stepped outside."

"I…I…You must understand. It's a busy time of year, my dearest Mina, when the wildflower meadows are in bloom, and we work hard to make our finest and most famous cheese, *Dumpling von der Wiese…*"

"Then why aren't these people out working, as well?"

"I…I…I thought we could spare this many. I wanted to welcome you, Mina. With a bit of a show. Like the old days," said Great-Uncle Frederik, hanging his head.

"I know you did, Uncle," I said, squeezing his hand and giving him a quick peck on the cheek. The photographer leaned in close for that! "And I know that Haunau-Brauncau has a great and glorious history…but that was then and this is now." I lifted my great-grandmother's coronet from my head and turned it in my hands. Really a lovely piece of jewellery, and how it glittered in the sunlight! "Perhaps you should sell this, Uncle, and use the money to do something nice for all these nice people."

"But…Mina…But…"

I turned back to the crowd, waved the coronet in the air, and yelled in a voice which would have done Amber proud on the hockey pitch, "The holiday begins now!"

"Hooray! Hooray! Long live Grand-Duchess Wilhemina Frederika! Hooray!"

The brass band, working hard to get the most sound out of their antique instruments, struck up the national anthem, a stirring tune with the almost unpronounceable title of "Ach, Was Für Eine Unglaublich Schöne Kuh," which translated, roughly, as "Oh, What a Lovely Cow You Are," and the people gathered in the square below began to dance. Great-Uncle Frederik, pouting like a fat baby, snatched the coronet out of my hand and jammed it back into his pocket, but I ignored him and kept waving at the Haunau-Braunkauvians, who laughed and chattered and danced and feasted the rest of the day…

This is the postcard that I sent to Amber, care of Wallywood School. One side had a picture taken from a mountainside meadow and featured a close-up of one of the local dairies, with the castle and town in the background far below. I made my great-uncle's chauffeur stop the Daimler before we reached the airport so that my card could catch the afternoon post.

"Dear Amber, Joseph, Zach, Miss Marquardt and everyone in Year 6…Had an *interesting* time in Haunau-Brauncau. It was great fun ruling the country for a day but somehow I have my doubts that I'll be choosing the name 'Frederika.' Tell you why when I get home. Off to St Petersburg. See you soon—Mina."

CHAPTER 5

St Petersburg is closer to the Arctic Circle than it is to the Equator, so in late May the evening twilight lingers a long time. Good thing, too, because there had been a delay in taking off from Munich, which meant I missed my connecting flight from Frankfurt to Moscow, and even though a very nice Russian lady put me on the next available flight, *that* flight was running four hours late coming in from Smolensk, and when it *did* finally land and refuel and board all its passengers and take off again, I honestly felt like the plane was powered by elastic bands and stuck together with cellotape. It was a terrible flight! The plane bumped and shuddered through storm-clouds, and the only food that the poor flight attendants had to offer was herring and caviar—which might sound posh, but herring is a slimy fish that's usually served raw, and caviar, in case you didn't know, is just salted fish eggs. Fish eggs! Honestly! Though I have to say that the other passengers were gobbling it all down like there was no tomorrow. Which perhaps there wasn't, given the storm and the appalling condition of the plane.

Thank goodness that Cousin Alexandra had indeed sent the ballet's private jet, as she'd promised, to meet me in Moscow and take me to St Petersburg—I was the only passenger, so I had the whole plane, and the entire refrigerator, to myself. Not a fish egg in sight, thank goodness. Not much more than celery sticks and cream crackers and diet cola to be had, alas—better than pickled herring, though!

As I staggered off the place at Pulkovo Airport, sleepy and still hungry, I noticed a tall, blond, incredibly thin, sad-looking gentleman holding a small cardboard sign which read, "Маленькая девочка для балета," which means, approximately, "little girl for ballet." I think. Thank goodness Mama had insisted I take Russian lessons while we were living in Uzbekistan that time…

"добрый день," I said, which means "Good afternoon." I think.

The sad-looking man smiled and bowed, so I smiled and bowed, and he told me his name was Ivan (I think) and ushered me through customs and bundled me into a huge square car called a Zil (I think), which looked like a big shiny black shoebox with wheels. And then we drove a long way, very slowly—Ivan was an exceptionally cautious driver. I must have fallen asleep, because I don't remember anything of the city until I awoke with a start to find that we'd stop outside the door of a colossal building, all grey stone and pillars and carved cornices and enormously tall windows hung with red velvet drapes: the Imperial Malakhov Theatre. Ivan opened the door of the Zil and gestured for me to go in.

Inside the lobby was a vast black and white marble floor, more pillars, more carvings, a gigantic curving staircase decorated with statues of all these pretty nymphs and

45

goddesses wearing nothing but draped bedclothes, looking very chilly, the poor things. The red carpeting on the steps was so thick I sank in up to my ankles. There was no one to be seen. It was all absolutely quiet. And a bit scary...

A couple of deep breaths, Mina!

I looked over my shoulder and saw Ivan (if that really was his name) smiling from the doorway, and pointing to the great carved doors at the top of the staircase. Reassured, I grabbed the gilded handle and pushed. They opened silently.

"No, no, no! You clumsy things!"

So much for silence. I'd recognise Cousin Alexandra's cat-like screech anywhere.

"The pose is wrong, wrong, wrong! The feet—like so! The arms—so!"

I crept forward and peered over the back row of seats. Far below me was a tiny square box of light, like a miniature television set—which I realised, after a moment, must be the stage, lit up for the afternoon's rehearsal. And those miniature figures moving about in the lighted box were actually full-sized grown-ups. The stage wasn't small, really—it was just that I was so far away from it.

Deep breaths, Mina! No use standing in the back of an enormous dark theatre, not when Cousin Alexandra was expected me. I started to walk down the aisle towards the stage. Her shrieking grew louder.

"The attitude—ah, how can I explain to you? The attitude must be…must be…uplifted! Inspired! Like a bird! Like a butterfly! Like an angel! Try it again! Again! Ah… No, no, no! Oh, I shall never make dancers of you! It's hopeless! Hopeless! Hopeless!"

And with a dramatic sigh, Cousin Alexandra collapsed onto the floorboards as the edge of the stage. She hadn't changed a bit since last December, really, though I have to say that she looked a good deal less interesting without her stage make-up on… Petite, perilously thin, her thick blonde hair scraped back into a messy chignon, wearing a black leotard and with her strong legs clad in worn grey tights. She was barefoot, and may I just say here and now that she had really ugly feet—bumpy and lumpy with corns and calluses everywhere. But that's what thirty years of dancing *en pointe* will do to you, I guess.

The chorus of dancers standing upstage took this opportunity to start whispering amongst themselves. Two or three of them pointed at me, standing in the front row of the house.

Cousin Alexandra turned to see what they were all looking at and immediately leaped to her feet. "Ah, Mina! Mina! Mina!" she cried, her arms spread wide and her usual (rather mad) grin on her face. "Welcome to the Imperial Malakhov Ballet! Ladies, make your bow to my dearest, sweetest little darling of a cousin!"

As if they'd rehearsed it—and hey, maybe they had—the chorus of ballerinas, as one, half-raised their arms and ever-so-gracefully sank into the deepest of curtseys. I sighed. Even dressed in rehearsal clothes, they were beautiful: thin, elegant, with high cheekbones, narrow, graceful necks and enormous eyes. If only Amber could see this! I thought.

But Cousin Alexandra was not so easily pleased, and she stormed along the line of dancers, correcting the placement of an arm here, the position of a foot there. "Hopeless! How you shame me! So clumsy! If only we had had longer to rehearse!"

"I thought it looked very pretty," I told Cousin Alexandra, and some of the ladies smiled hesitantly.

"Ah, you are a dear, sweet girl, Mina—but 'pretty' isn't good enough! 'Pretty' is for amateurs! It must be beautiful! It must be perfect! It must be magnificent!"

"Why?"

"Why? Because this is the Imperial Malakhov! Because tonight is the premiere of my new ballet, *The Swan and the Summer Stars*. Because the entire world will be watching us tonight!" And she struck a pose which reminded me of the marble nymph-ladies on the staircase in the lobby.

A bit silly, I thought, but aloud I said only, "Really, Cousin Alexandra? The entire world?

Cousin Alexandra dropped her pose and spoke in a much more normal voice. "Well, the entire *ballet* world. And

48

that's really the only part that matters, isn't it?" Her dancers all nodded in agreement and whispered amongst themselves.

"Ah, how they shall marvel!" Cousin Alexandra went on, striding confidently along the line of dancers, with me alongside, scurrying to keep up. "So bold a dance...so daring...so modern...so important!"

"Well," I asked from behind, "if it's so important, why haven't you been rehearsing it longer?"

Cousin Alexandra stopped as if she'd been slapped. I almost ran into her backside. "How could we? When we were all waiting for our star dancer to appear?" And she stared at me with a strange, hungry, over-excited look in her eye, which was instantly mirrored by every woman on the stage.

I suddenly had a very bad feeling about this... "And who might that be?"

"Why, you, my dear cousin!"

I gulped. "Me?" My voice came out as a squeak.

"But of course!" cried Cousin Alexandra, striking another one of her poses. "I created this new ballet just for you!"

My stomach felt as if someone had punched me, and hard. "But—but—but Cousin Alexandra, I'm not a ballet dancer!"

"What? Of course you are! You're my cousin, aren't you? Dancing is in your blood!"

"It most certainly is *not*!"

"Don't be ridiculous, my dear! Why, how well I remember all those family gatherings on the Riviera, when you were a little girl, and how you would twirl across the room on your toes, delighting all the party guests!"

"Cousin Alexandra, I was two years old! I could barely walk!"

She brushed my distress aside with a single sweeping gesture. "And I know you had lessons after that. I insisted that your mother arrange it."

"Yes, she did," I told her frantically. "But that was at Mrs. Cottlington's School of Tap and Jazz, upstairs from the greengrocer's shop in the High Street in Royal Tunbridge Wells! It was never anything like the Imperial Malakhov Ballet!"

"No matter, no matter, no matter! I'm sure it will all come back to you. Here, put this on." She snapped her fingers and one of the ballerinas ran over with a white tutu which she wedged on somehow over my blue jeans. "Charming! Now, I'll leave you to run through the opening while I make a few telephone calls. The curtain goes up in three hours, and I must notify the press to expect something magical!"

Three hours? I'd've been just as horrified if it had been three days—three months—three years! "Cousin Alexandra, wait—you've got to listen to me! I can't—I don't—"

"Three hours, dear! Now, you and you and you," she shrilled, pointing. "Show her the steps. Teach her the

50

combinations. Simple, yes?" And Cousin Alexandra swept off as if she'd been wearing a ball gown, and I found myself left alone on that enormous bare stage with three dozen desperately skinny young women who began to push and pull at me, trying to get me to do what they were doing.

PAS DE CHAT,
CHANGEMENT,
PAS DE CHAT,
CHANGEMENT.
ARABESQUE RIGHT AND HOLD.
ARABESQUE LEFT AND HOLD.
POINT AND POINT AND POINT
AND PIROUETTE ONE
AND PIROUETTE TWO
AND POSE, EXTEND THE ARM AND HOLD.

I was twirled about, stage right, stage left, upstage, downstage, until I was dizzy. I could hardly recall anything that Mrs Cottlington had taught me when I was five years old, and what little Russian I remembered from three years ago had completely drained from my brain. "Do any of you speak English?" I begged, but if any of them did, they weren't going to admit it, not when Cousin Alexandra had told them to teach me...

PAS DE CHAT,

CHANGEMENT,

PAS DE CHAT,

CHANGEMENT.

ARABESQUE RIGHT AND HOLD.

(PLIE AND POINT, PLIE AND POINT)

ARABESQUE LEFT AND HOLD.

(PLIE AND POINT, PLIE AND POINT)

POINT AND POINT AND POINT

AND POINT AND POINT AND POINT

AND PIROUETTE ONE

AND PIROUETTE TWO

AND POSE, EXTEND THE ARM AND HOLD.

And after two impossibly sweaty hours I found myself bundled off the stage, tugged and pushed and pulled through dusty, grimy hallways and down noisy metal staircases, past gurgling hot-water pipes—oh, the Imperial Malkhov Theatre might look super-fancy from out front, but that was for the paying customers, not the performers—to a crowded, over-bright dressing room, where rows and rows of anorexic-looking ballerinas applied layers and layers of pancake makeup and red slashes of lipstick and quarter-inch-wide stripes of eyeliner. They looked rather ridiculous—and scary. Two of them plonked me into a chair in front of a mirror lined with scorching white light-bulbs and did the same thing to me, however much I kept protesting. Someone else brought me a plate of dry crackers and more celery sticks and a glass of fizzy water and murmured, "Here is some dinner for you," while the rest of the corps de ballet stared at the food with envious, ravenous eyes...

Then I was zipped and pinned and buttoned somehow into ice-blue leotard and tights, and thrust into a tutu made of sky-blue ostrich feathers, and the same two ballerinas were hurrying me back up the noisy metal staircases and past the gurgling hot-water pipes and through the dusty, grimy hallways, and onto the stage, and there was music swelling into shivering climaxes from an orchestra I couldn't see because there were two blinding spotlights in my eyes, and Cousin Alexandra was standing there, in a beautiful pose, her heavily made-up face noble, her arms stretched out in supplication, waiting for me to begin to dance... I half-heartedly raised my arms in mimicry of hers, then...

"No," I said. I dropped my arms. "This is stupid. I won't do it."

Cousin Alexandra's face never changed expression, but her eyes widened. "Mina!" she whispered frantically, her mouth barely moving. "Mina, please! The audience is waiting."

"No! I won't do it. I refuse. You're the ballet dancer, Cousin Alexandra, not me!"

Cousin Alexandra stiffened for a moment, then let loose a silvery little laugh as she improvised a perfect little

53

spin which brought her to my side, where she could hiss into my ear.

"Nonsense, my dearest niece! Dancing is in your blood! How well I remember when I came to your first ballet recital! How adorable you looked in your pink dress and darling little fairy wings! And when you took your bow, how you ran to me and kissed my cheek and told me how you wanted to be a prima ballerina, just like me!"

"I was five years old!" I sputtered. "Every girl wants to be a ballerina when she's five years old! But I'm not five years old now and I know perfectly well that this is just another stupid bribe and all you really want is for me to choose your name...and I'm not having it!"

And I wriggled out of that stupid blue tutu, threw it to the floor, and stormed offstage, leaving Cousin Alexandra frozen in the glare of the spotlights. As I reached the noisy metal staircase that led down to the dressing rooms, I did notice that there seemed to be a great deal of noise coming from the audience...Applause? Why should anyone be applauding? But I didn't care. In the deserted dressing room I wiped my face clean, found my clothes and my travel bag, and blundered my way through various side corridors until I found myself in the lobby—where I discovered Ivan (if that was really his name) waiting for me. "Let's go, I told him, "before Cousin Alexandra can find me and put me in another tutu."

As we were escaping, the people working behind the lobby bars began popping the corks on bottles of champagne. Audience members, the ladies in evening gowns and jewels and the gentlemen in tuxedoes began to exit the auditorium, all of them chatting loudly and variously in French and English and Russian. I understood most of it, I think.

"Amazing!" said one elderly woman dripping with sables and rubies, "Truly, I've never seen anything like it!"

Her companion nodded reverently. "So bold... so daring... so modern... so important!"

"Such vision! Such talent! However does Lyps-Hyanova do it?"

"Why, it's—it's positively revolutionary!" trumpeted another man, who was tapping away at the tiny keyboard of his mobile phone. "A dancer who refuses to dance! A dance about *not* dancing! So new! So fresh! So—so radical! I must send my review to *Balletomania* immediately! Lyps-Hyanova is a *genius*!"

I left Cousin Alexandra there, centre stage, curtseying to her adoring public, being showered with red roses while the applause went on and on....

Before Ivan escorted me back to the Zil and drove me back to the airport, I managed to post another card back to Wallywood:

55

"Dear Amber, Joseph, Zach and everyone—Hope you like this photo of the Hermitage Museum! Not that I had time to see it while I was in St Petersburg, but Ivan says that it's pretty impressive. At least, I think that's what he's saying. I made quite an impression at the ballet, but it's all much too complicated to tell you about in a postcard. Let me just say that I don't think that I'll be choosing the name 'Alexandra.' Off to Monte Carlo to visit Cousin Antoine. Miss you! Mina."

CHAPTER SIX

Getting *out* of Russia was as tedious as getting *into* Russia. Endless delays at the airports! I fell sound asleep on the flight from St Petersburg to Moscow, and again on the overnight flight from Moscow to the south of France, awakening as the plane touched down at Aéroport Nice Côte d'Azur. It was very early on a beautiful May morning, already brimming with glorious Mediterranean sunshine. I do love being by the sea! I always feel as if I could cup the warm, salty air in my two hands as if it were water, and splash my face with it.

This time, it wasn't a chauffeur waiting, but Cousin Antoine himself, dashing as ever, his bronze-coloured hair perfectly cut, his tall, slim frame impeccably dressed, an orange scarf tied at the throat of his spotless white shirt.

"Mina! *Ma très chère cousine*," he announced loudly and cheerfully as ticket agents and other passengers pointed and whispered. "*Parfaitement!* You are just in time! Did you bring your goggles?"

I'd napped on my journey, but not enough, apparently. Could I be hearing Cousin Antoine correctly? "My what?"

"Your goggles, my dear cousin, your goggles! You can't attend the racing without goggles!"

Yes, evidently that's exactly what he'd said before. "Uh...I didn't know that I was going to be attending any racing, Cousin Antoine."

"But of *course* you are attending the racing!" he laughed, as he hurried me towards his car—a bright orange Lamborghini, illegally parked on the double yellow lines just outside the door. "What else is there to do in Monte Carlo, in May? Everyone goes to the racing! Now, you will be riding with me! A special treat!" There was a policeman hovering by the car, but instead of giving Cousin Antoine a parking ticket, he asked for an autograph instead, which my cousin signed with his usual flourish and a cheeky grin.

"He seems to know who you are, Cousin Antoine. Did you see? He practically bowed!"

"Everyone on the Côte d'Azur knows Antoine LaVitesse, *ma chère*!" He chuckled as he wedged my suitcase into the tiny space behind the driver's seat. "And because you are my cousin, and because it is the morning of the race, they will soon be bowing to you, too, my dear!

"The race?" I really did still feel half-asleep.

"The Grand Prix de Monte Carlo! Perfect timing! Aren't you lucky? So, are we ready? Are we buckled in? *Alors, viens!* Let's go!"

And we tore away from the kerb with a jolt and a squeal of tyres. The blue, blue waters of the Mediterranean glittered on our right, and on the left the mountains climbed to the blue, blue sky above us—and what I remembered from a few years before as a lovely hillside covered with groves of olive trees and tangles of wildflowers was now almost completely covered with houses and gated residential compounds and towering blocks of flats, all in tints of white and cream and pink and blue, all with enormous balconies and terraces overlooking the sea.

"Gosh, Cousin Antoine, it's changed a lot around here. So many new houses!"

"But of course, my dear cousin—who would not want to live in such a beautiful part of the world?"

Beautiful? Well, maybe to some people. Myself, I think I preferred the look of the olive trees and flowers which had graced the hillsides for so many hundreds of years...

Even so early in the morning, the roadway, twisting and turning among the houses, was dense with traffic, but Cousin Antoine's car magically seemed to find open spaces where other, more commonplace cars, could not hope to do so. Cousin Antoine changed lanes with skilful little flicks to the steering wheel and gear-shift, all the while keeping up a running commentary on the places we were passing and the people who lived there: "Monsieur Oliphant's mansion. More money than taste, that one. If only he'd hired Yvonne, my personal interior designer, as I advised him. Expensive, of course, but she is worth every *centime*," and "There, below, my dear friend Eloise Cordonbleue's new yacht. So large, so pretentious! She has invited us for drinks, after the race. She is in love with me, of course, *pauvre petite*. But then, they all are."

"Uh, Cousin Antoine, could we slow down a little?"

I thought that we were going to crash at least a dozen times, but somehow we never did.

"*Pas possible*, Mina. We don't want to be late, now do we?"

Late? For what? Our own funerals?

Before I knew it, we were in and out of Cousin Antoine's enormous luxury flat, located on what he assured me was the most exclusive street in Monte Carlo. It had the most amazing view of the harbour and the sea beyond it, but I scarcely had time to step out onto the balcony before I was whisked away by some of Cousin Antoine's "people," who hurriedly dressed me in an orange jumpsuit and helmet (to match those being worn by Cousin Antoine), all the while jabbering away at me in such quick French that I could hardly keep up.

"Cousin Antoine, I don't have a very clear picture of what's going on here…"

We were something that people were calling "the pit" (they pronounced it as "le peeeet"), a busy and confusing place with lots of men hurrying here and there and yelling at each other in at least six languages. I heard French, German, Italian, Spanish, plus others I couldn't recognise, in addition to English from both England and America. There was a horrid stink of petrol and all these strange-looking machines resembling like giant insects, shiny with new paint and covered with decals from manufacturers and industrial companies, being off-loaded from enormous lorries. Cars, I realised, but not like any cars you'd ever see on the streets. *Racing* cars...

"And there she is, my dear Mina!" cried Cousin Antoine proudly, waving his white-gloved hand at one of the science-fiction-movie-looking cars. It was low and sleek and glowed with bright orange paint, which seemed to be Cousin Antoine's signature colour. "My custom-built MacCammack Formula One, complete with the finest, most powerful DuGuépard engine in the world! Notice the second seat."

I *had* noticed. "And that's for—?"

"For you, dear cousin! As I told you at the airport, today you are riding with me!"

"But I thought—"

Uh-oh.

Now, I realise that someone like Zach would have leapt at the privilege. Joseph would have thought it an incredible, once-in-a-lifetime opportunity. I think even Mr Patel would have appreciated it more than I could! Because all I felt was scared. No, not just scared—terrified!

I mean, wouldn't you? Those race cars may look big and imposing when you're standing next to one, but once you're strapped into their tiny, tiny seats, so snug that your bottom hardly has room to wriggle, and once you're moving at close to one hundred miles an hour with all these other absolutely insane drivers trying to get ahead of you... Believe me, that big powerful car feels as flimsy as a hand-made go-kart.

"Cousin Antoine, do my mother and father know about this? Did they say it was okay for me to race with you today?"

"But of course! I telephoned them this morning—well, it was early, and I had to leave a message..."

Uh-oh, again.

Cars pushed into position by big burly men, ours in the "pole position," which, apparently, was the very best place to be. No one bothered to tell me why. Cameras flashing. Through the narrow opening of my helmet I could see only straight ahead, where a man stood solemnly with a silk flag on a stick.

Cousin Antoine reached into his chest pocket and drew out a small, well-worn leather wallet, opened it and stared down at something—a little black-and-white photograph, I thought—for a moment. Then he raised it to his lips, kissed it, and replaced it in his pocket before turning back to me with a cheeky grin and giving me a thumbs-up.

"What was that picture, Cousin Antoine?" I asked above the steady hubbub of the crowd and the deep growl of all the engines.

"My guardian angel!" he laughed nonchalantly, and then the man holding the flag started waving it. And with a roar and a squeal of burning rubber, we were off.

Monaco is a tiny country, not even one square mile in size—I've been on golf courses with Daddy that covered more ground—and the course of the Grand Prix seems to twist and turn up and down every single one of its frighteningly narrow and curvy streets, past all these churches and hotels and blocks of flats where crowds of fans scream encouragement and wave flags showing the colours of their favourite drivers. I noticed orange flags everywhere... All right, so the entire course is only about two miles long, but there's this one impossible hairpin twist in the road, where we kept skidding sideways before Cousin Antoine could bring the car back under control, and there's this tunnel where one second you're blinded by darkness and then the next, as you exit it, you're blinded by the sunlight. All the while the tyres humming and the engines roaring and the crowds cheering, all the sounds merging in one huge cacophony of sound, like an untuned orchestra... I swear that Cousin Antoine was singing along to it...

SWERVING, WHEELING
TYRES SQUEALING
ENGINES ROARING
CROWDS ADORING
A LOVELY DAY

DOWN THE STRAIGHTAWAY
NOW THROUGH THE CURVE
WE SPIN AND SWERVE

C'EST MERVEILLEUX!
C'EST TOUT PARFAIT!
WATCH LAVITESSE
WIN ONE MORE DAY!
C'EST VRAI! BIEN FAIT!

And you have to do seventy-eight laps of that silly impractical miniature country. One hundred and sixty-two miles.

Cousin Antoine and I did it in a little over an hour. A new record, apparently.

Hooray for us.

C'EST MERVEILLEUX!
C'EST TOUT PARFAIT!
WATCH LAVITESSE
WIN ONE MORE DAY!
HIP-HIP- HOORAY!
C'EST VRAI! BIEN FAIT!

I wish that I could tell you more about it, but to be honest I had my eyes closed for almost the entire time.

Occasionally we'd pull over for more petrol or for a tyre change, but these pit stops never seem to last more than a couple of heartbeats before we were off again. I could see Cousin Antoine grinning a wild grin and shouting something gleefully into the wind as the orange MacCammack shrieked through curves and roared down straight-aways, but I couldn't hear him over the noise of the engine and I know he couldn't hear me as I prayed (and prayed and prayed) for the race to be over.

And finally—finally!—my prayers were answered. There was a checquered flag whipping about in a figure-eight pattern, and sometime soon after that the car shuddered to a halt. There was cheering—massive amounts of it. There were people in orange jumpsuits mobbing the car, pulling Cousin Antoine and me from the choke-hold of those impossibly cramped seats and thrusting us up onto a box in front of what seemed like hundreds of flashing cameras and shouting reporters. Cousin Antoine was in his glory, smiling and waving as a trophy was thrust into his hands.

"Merci!" he shouted, holding it above his head. "Thank you! Thank you! *Merci!* It is thrilling to win yet another Grand Prix here in beautiful Monte Carlo! And just let me say that this has been a very special race for me, as I was accompanied through its many twists and turns by my dear little cousin Mina *Antoinette* Jones—say hello to the nice people, Mina! Smile,

dear, smile! This is for the front page of *Le Monde* newspaper! And now this one is for *F1 Racing*..."

"Hello—"

"And I am certain that Mina will join me in congratulating the other drivers who were just a *tiny* bit slower and less skillful than I in navigating this oh-so-tricky course. Better luck next time, that is how you say it *en anglais,* eh, Mina?"

"Yes, better luck—"

"And of course I'd like to thank my devoted sponsors, Helium Brand Tyres and Speed-Demon Brand Racing Petrol. We could not have done it without them, could we, Mina?"

"I suppose not, but—"

"And finally I feel I must give full honours to the devoted team of mechanics that keeps my magnificent MacCammack racing machine on the road. Thanks to Nicolas and Micky and Eduard and Alain and Tomaso and Brad. Also to Harry and Louis and Mathieu and Pierre and Hans and Dieter and Aloysius and Lorenzo and Paul and David, and, of course, to Coco and Connie and Helinka in the office, and Myron and Sandy and Dennis and Lars up in Manchester, and to Jules and Jim and Justin and Jenny and Joanne in publicity, and to Sir Edmund Lollipop for his faithful financial support over the years, *and et, bien sûr, à ma mère et mon père, et à mes sœurs Marie et Marthe et Madeleine et mes frères David et Philippe et Robert et Gary et Michel* —"

"Cousin Antoine?"

"*Silence*, Mina—And where would I be without my devoted team of hairdressers and personal appearance specialists? So thanks to Lulu and Miriamne and Katherine and Alicia and to Mr. Samson and Troy and Erik in the tailoring department for designing my fabulous racing outfits, which incidentally are available for purchase at Boutique Vitesse on rue DeCoupage—"

"Cousin Antoine? I really have—"

"Quiet, Mina!—and above all, I would like to thank you, my devoted fans, for your continued support as I win trophy after trophy after trophy—"

"Cousin Antoine? Cousin Antoine! I'm leaving."

"What? What?" Cousin Antoine turned his head this way and that, smiling and posing as the cameras flashed and flashed and flashed. "Did I miss something? Does someone need to take my photograph? Did someone want my autograph? Did someone say something important?"

"No," I said quietly, slipping away through the crowd. "No one said anything important."

I found a postcard with a pretty view of Monaco's harbour, packed as tight as sardines in a can with the glittering white yachts of the rich and famous. I circled the one that belonged to Cousin Antoine's friend Mme Cordonbleue.

"Dear Amber, Joseph, and Zach—This is the boat where I'm *not* drinking champagne tonight! The Grand Prix was quite an experience—I don't think I want to drive above 30 miles per hour ever again as long as I live. I doubt that I'll be choosing the name 'Antoinette,' unless my other relatives are even worse. And they might be! *Je pars pour Paris dans quelques minutes*— that means 'I leave for Paris in a few minutes.' Wish me luck! Mina."

CHAPTER 7

Have you ever been to Paris? It is one of my very favourite places in the whole wide world. There is so much to do and so much to see—churches, museums, concerts, shopping—but what I like best is simply to walk around—to *flâner*, as the French would say, to stroll about. I like wandering aimlessly, turning down any street that looks interesting, daydreaming about items in displays—*lecher-les-vitrines* they call it, "to lick the windows," which sounds gross when you first hear it but then makes a sort of sense, especially when you've stopped in front of some fabulous bakery or pastry shop—and stopping whenever I get footsore in some charming little café. Mama and I used to spend whole days doing just that… There's a drink you can get called a *citron pressé*, which is a sort of really tart lemonade, and another one I like called a *diabolo*, which is minty and refreshing on a hot summer's day.

That Friday I had both.

I hadn't been able to leave Monaco as early as I would have liked. I was supposed to stay overnight, but in the glow of winning the Grand Prix, it appeared as though Cousin Antoine had completely forgotten my existence. Typical…

One of his assistants (Margo? Marthe? Marianne?) took me to the train station and booked a ticket for me, but Cousin Antoine had also forgotten that he was supposed to put me on the TGV, the super-fast train that zips around France at about 200 miles per hour. Just as well, really, as I'd had my fill of traveling really, *really* fast... The slow train left Monaco station about 8:30 that night, and stopped at Nice, then Antibes, then Cannes, then a couple of tiny towns I can't remember, then Toulon... and then I fell asleep, and didn't wake up until the train pulled into Gare Austerlitz at eight o'clock in the morning.

I could have telephoned my aunts, I suppose. I could have taken *le Métro*, which is what the Parisians call their underground train system, or waited in the queue for a taxi. But Mama and Daddy and I had lived in Paris for the better part of a year when I was nine, when Daddy was lecturing in engineering at the Sorbonne, and no self-respecting Parisian girl of eleven years of age would think twice about crossing the city on her own, *sans adultes*—without any adults, that is... so I walked.

Call it "pluck," as Great-Aunt Wilhemina likes to say... "My plucky girl!"

I love it when she says that. I like being her plucky girl.

Old songs and movies always go on and on about "April in Paris," but there's nothing wrong with the city in May, as far as I'm concerned. It was a beautiful morning, clear and fresh. The Jardin des Plantes, which is a lovely little botanical garden, was just opening, so I strolled along the neat fenced-in beds of herbs and exotic vegetation, nodding "bonjour" to the gardeners and to all the animals in the little menagerie. The elephant lifted its trunk and trumpeted a greeting back.

I threaded the colourful tangle of streets that is the Latin Quarter, stopping for a croissant and a hot chocolate on the Rue Mouffetard, a frantically busy shopping street, closed to vehicles, where you can buy anything from a single strawberry to a Persian carpet to four hundred different types of cheeses, or so the sign in the window of one *fromagerie*—a cheese shop—claimed, without exaggerating, I think.

I walked past my old school—through the window, pasted high up on the walls of the infants' room, I could see dozens of colourful finger-paintings, and hear them singing that song about dancing on the bridge in Avignon.

Then it was up past the great big fancy white dome of the Panthéon and along Rue Soufflot, where the university students hang out and drink endless coffees and discuss philosophy in loud, passionate voices, and into the Jardin du Luxembourg, an enormous formal park, with chestnut trees growing in rigid rows and vast beds of marigolds and pansies outlining long rectangular ponds. I treated myself to another *chocolat chaud* at the café by the Medici Fountain, fortifying myself for the upcoming visit with my aunts…

Paris, in case you didn't know, is divided up into twenty sections called *arrondisements*, which spiral out from Notre-Dame Cathedral at the centre in a pattern like the shell of a snail. Auntie Persimmon and Auntie Sylvia lived on opposite sides of a small, elegant and very exclusive little square in the expensive sixth arrondisement, not very far from where I was enjoying my hot chocolate, but I wasn't planning on ringing either of their doorbells—not before eleven o'clock anyway, as that would be very likely to disturb their beauty sleep. No, I planned to wait until lunchtime, when they'd be holding court at their favourite cafés: La Plume (which translates as "the feather" but means "the pen," I guess from the days when people used to dip goose quills into pots of ink to write their letters), Auntie Persimmon's brasserie of choice, directly across the street from L'Etoile, which means "the star"—and where else could you possibly expect Auntie Sylvia to eat her lunch?

The bell in one of the tall, not-quite-twin towers of St Sulpice—a really enormous church, one of the biggest in Paris, second in size only to the great cathedral of Notre-Dame—was solemnly tolling out one o'clock as I walked serenely towards the complicated knot of little streets just beyond the busy Boulevard St Germain. Well, maybe "serenely" is stretching the truth a bit…although as I stood in a crowd of businessmen and businesswomen and students waiting to cross the Boulevard, I told myself (and told myself, and told myself) that lunch with Auntie Persimmon and Auntie Sylvia couldn't be worse that standing on a huge stage in a blue tutu or driving around Monaco at one hundred miles an hour, could it?

72

Of course it could.

Deep breath, Mina! Deep breath…And one more…

There was a smile on my face as I turned the corner on rue des Jumelles. It was immediately obvious that Auntie Persimmon and Auntie Sylvia were already seating at their usual tables across the street from each other, and holding court for the usual small army of photographers, fans and autograph seekers. Auntie Persimmon caught my eye a fraction of a second before her sister did, and beckoned me with one diamond-bedecked hand to take the seat across from her at La Plume. Her personal secretary, Mademoiselle Azulai, a slender, frightened-face woman dressed in a chic black suit, her dark eyes edged with a thin line of kohl, was perched on the edge of a chair to my right, and there was a tall, thin, bleached-looking man with a huge camera sitting on my left.

"Mina! DAHLING!" purred Auntie Persimmon, kissing the air in the vicinity of both my cheeks. "Mwah! Mwah! Oh, don't you look lovely, *lovely*, LOVELY!"

Lovely? After an all-night train journey and a nothing but a hurried scrub of the face and brush of the hair in a tiny train bathroom? But—"Thank you, Auntie Persimmon. It's so nice to see you again."

You couldn't really say the same for her—"lovely," I mean—though anyone would have to admit that she was striking-looking. She was wearing one of her voluminous purple silk dress-caftan-things and a wide-brimmed floppy hat and her usual array of glittery bracelets and bangles and beaded necklaces, her bejeweled spectacles on beaded string around her neck. Purply-red lipstick and purply-blue eyeshadow and thick black mascara. Curly, curly, curly jet-black hair—a little too curly, and a little too black, if you know what I mean. She *had* to be dyeing it…A bit over-the-top, you might think, like an actress who was playing the part of an eccentric writer…but then you noticed how her sharp black eyes darted here, flickered there, missing nothing—and sure enough, there was a little purple leather notebook a few inches from her right hand. Auntie Persimmon noticed *everything*—every person walking by, every car trying to maneuver into a tiny parking space, every pigeon fluttering on every window-ledge—and if it was important enough, she wrote it down. You never knew what—or who—might end up in one of her novels.

"DAHLING girl!" she murmured, leaning over the table and patting the back of my hand. My goodness, that diamond had to be the size of a peach-pit! Her books must be selling well… "You remember Mademoiselle Azulai, of course? My right ARM! My BOSWELL! I couldn't manage withOUT her. And this is—this is—" Her hands waved about in the air, as if to summon his name from an external memory source. "THIS is a lovely man from *The Times* or—or—or some such paper. They're doing a special FEATURE on me, you know, for the Sunday MAGAZINE! To be read by MILLIONS!"

She really did talk that way. You could hear the capital letters in her voice.

"Now, DAHLING, you must be EXHAUSTED! All this dashing about the continent! TEDIOUS old Frederik and egoTIStical Antoine and that GHASTLY scatter-brained Alexandra showing NO consideration for your YOUTH and DELICACY! Your parents ought to have sent you here to me in Paris IMMEDIATELY!" And she patted my hand again—I could see her other hand twitching, itching to take notes.

"It's been all right, Auntie Persimmon," I assured her. "A bit of an adventure, really."

"Well, you must be STARVING! Let's order luncheon AT ONCE!"

"I thought I might go and see Auntie Sylvia first—"

"Don't even MENTION that name, DAHLING! I can't TELL you the indignities that I have SUFFERED because of that WOMAN!" Just then the mobile phone—which looked gold-plated to me—lying next to the purple notebook burbled, chirruping out the love theme from the film version of one of Auntie Persimmon's bestsellers, *The Other Side of Tonight*. Auntie Persimmon glared at it. "GET that, Agnès. And tell her I'm EXTREMELY busy at the moment!"

"No, really, Auntie Persimmon, I'll just pop over to say hello—"

"But NOT before this LOVELY man takes your PHOTOGRAPH!" she trilled. "Come sit here by me! Move,

75

Agnès," she added in a growled undertone, and poor little Mademoiselle Azulai scooted over to an empty chair. The mobile phone kept burbling. "I DID say to GET that, *DEAR!*" Mademoiselle Azulai snatched up the phone and cowered away from us, murmuring an apologetic "Allo?" as the skinny man from *The Times* (or wherever) snapped shot after shot...

"Auntie Persimmon, if I could just dash across—"

"But we haven't ordered LUNCHEON yet, darling!" Auntie Persimmon was the only person I knew who said "luncheon" instead of calling it plain old lunch. "I was THINKING of lobster SALAD—*salade des homards, s'il vous plait,*" she fluted to a hovering waiter. "That's lobster salad, you know. And CHAMPAGNE—for us, of course. What will you have, Mina, dear?"

"*Citron pressé, s'il vous plait,*" I said politely, giving the waiter a smile. "And now, Auntie Persimmon—"

"I know, I KNOW, my love, you run along and pay your respects to that WOMAN over there! If you must, you MUST! But before you go—" and she leaned in close and covered one of my hands with one of hers. "Before you go, a word of advice. Your Auntie Prue—oh, SYLVIA, I suppose we must call her!—she will stop at NOTHING to get you to choose her name. NOTHING! I am SERIOUS, child! The most underhanded, devious—well, it's how she's made her name and fortune, after ALL. So BEWARE!"

I gently slid my hand out from under Auntie Persimmon's. "Thanks. I'm sure I'll be okay."

Auntie Persimmon's sharp black eyes fastened on me. "NOT that I want you to choose MY name, of course!" she laughed lightly—and falsely. I could tell. Anyone could tell! "I SIMPLY don't want you to choose HERS! That would be intoler—MOST unsuitable!"

I just smiled and slipped out of my seat, checking both ways for speeding motor-scooters before I stepped off the kerb—oh! "Curb," you'd say back in the United States. Sounds the same, though.

"Don't be LONG, dear one!" trilled Auntie Persimmon in a voice you could have heard back in Monaco. "Our lobster will be here in a MOMENT! And if you're a VERY good girl, you MIGHT get a sip of my CHAMPAGNE!"

But I don't even like champagne, I thought to myself as I approached the crowded terrace outside L'Etoile. It tastes sour and the bubbles go up my nose... I glanced back at La Plume and saw Auntie Persimmon already scribbling frantically in her purple notebook. Just then her mobile started burbling again. So did Mademoiselle Azulai's. So did the photographers. Burple-twitter-chime—very musical! Like some sort of new sort of electronic orchestra...

(BURBLE)

DAHLING!

77

(GURBLE)

ALLO?

(BUZZ—BUZZ)

MAIS OUI!

WHO IS—?

THAT WAS—?

DAHLING! SWEETHEART!

ALLO? MAIS NON!

(JINGLE)

MON CHER!

(RINGLE)

WHO'S THERE?

ALLO? MAIS OUI!

MAIS PAS AUJOURD'HUI

COMPLETELY BOOKED!

ANOTHER DAY?

(GLOOP-GLOOP)

SHALL WE SAY

A WEEK TOMORROW?

MORE CHAMPAGNE!

(BUZZ-BUZZ)

WHO IS—?

WHO WAS—?

LOBSTER! *HOMARD!*

MORE CHAMPAGNE?

NOW, MINA, DAHLING

ABOUT YOUR NAME…

But I was safely across the narrow street and the sounds of those mobiles and those voices were fading behind me. Still, one voice out of the multiple conversations threaded its way through to my ear:

I MIGHT PUT YOU IN A NOVEL,
OR IMMORTALISE YOU IN VERSE!
YOU NEEDN'T CHOOSE *MY* NAME,
JUST DON'T CHOOSE *HERS*…

CHAPTER EIGHT

Auntie Sylvia was surrounded by people, too, more than in Auntie Persimmon's little entourage. No personal assistant, true—she sat regally alone under her umbrella. But no fewer than *three* waiters poised nearby, practically twitching, watching and waiting to fulfill her slightest desire, plus the *sommelier* with the wine list, and at least six or seven people at nearby tables trying to get up the nerve to approach the great lady and ask for an autograph…and photographers, at least five of them, lingering, hovering, leaning in doorways with telephoto lenses on their cameras, the paparazzi circling like hungry hawks, waiting for the one perfect shot…

I knew it must be driving Auntie Persimmon crazy.

Because, although however popular Auntie Persimmon's books might be, however many she wrote and sold, however famous she was, Auntie Sylvia had always gone one better. She wasn't merely famous—oh, no, Auntie Sylvia was a *star*. The words "star power" might have been invented to describe her.

Black, black hair—just as suspiciously black as her sister's, but cut into a sleek, chic Parisian bob. The reddest of red lipstick, a slash of colour across her pale, beautiful face. An expensive little black suit with a red silk rose pinned to the lapel, and a matching bloom pinned to her impossibly tiny and stylish little hat. Dark glasses hiding her famous sultry eyes.

Her red, red nails were tapping impatiently at the stem of her wine glass.

She arched one perfect eyebrow as I leaned down to kiss her cheek.

"*Dearest* girl," she purred, deep in her throat, a feline smile playing about her perfect lips. "I was *wondering* when that *woman* would release you from her *inconsequential* conversation and free you to visit with *me*."

Whereas Auntie Persimmon seemed to speak in capital letters, Auntie Sylvia preferred the subtlety of *italics*—her words were always weighted down with *significant meaning*.

"After all, we *do* have something *serious* to discuss. But *first*—a bit of lunch." And she snapped her fingers at one of the hovering waiters, who leapt at once to her side, quivering with willingness, pad and pencil at the ready. She smiled—Auntie Sylvia *loves* it when people pay attention to her.

"Oh, but Auntie Persimmon has already—"

Auntie Sylvia pretended not to hear. "Champagne, of course, *darling*. Vintage Veuve Clicquot. Well *iced*," she cautioned in a carefully modulated murmur which could, no doubt, be heard by everyone else in the café, and probably by everyone sitting across the street at La Plume. "Something cool and sweet for my *darling* niece. And *salade des homards*, I think, to start."

"That's exactly what Auntie Persimmon ordered—"

"And, of course," she hurried on, "your finest *pâté de foie gras* and some of those *delightful* vols-au-vents that Pierre makes so well." Auntie Sylvia lowered her sunglasses a fraction and smiled at the waiter, who came close to swooning, no doubt dazzled by the nearness of his favourite screen goddess—or perhaps just really, really pleased that his customer had ordered several hundred euros' worth of lunch at one go. He hurried away, and Auntie Sylvia turned that famous, high-wattage, movie-star smile on me. "*Nothing* is too good for my namesake," she said sweetly.

And falsely. I could tell. Anyone could tell!

And I don't even like *pâté de foie gras.* In case you've never been asked by some desperate-to-impress-you person to taste some, it looks like pinky-brown peanut butter and it's made of liver. *Liver!* Really! I have never understood why someone would even bother to try to make an expensive luxury food item out of *liver*...

"Now, Mina, dear, while we're waiting to be served, we must have a little chat. I feel that it's my aunt ly duty to tell you—"

Just then her mobile phone started to chime, a sound like distant church bells. Auntie Sylvia glared at its tiny screen in irritation.

"Do you need to answer that, Auntie Sylvia?"

"*No.* Stupid thing! I only left it on in case my *agent* called about this new *film*—how*ever* did she get this number?"

"Who, Aunt?"

"That *woman* across the street. Your Auntie *Persimmon. Tire*some creature! So *rude*! Phoning during *luncheon*..."

So Auntie Sylvia used the word, too!

"Well, we'll soon get *this* sorted!" Tearing off her sunglasses impatiently, and with a moue of distaste on her perfect mouth, Auntie Sylvia poked at a button on her phone and held it to her porcelain cheek. "What is it, Persimmon, *dear*? Mina and I are just about to have our lunch..."

A moment later she had to hold the phone six or eight inches away from her ear, as Auntie Persimmon's displeased reply could be heard from across the street as well as through Auntie Sylvia's phone.

"I'm just calling to TELL you, Sylvia DEAR, that Mina's lunch is on the TABLE and I expect her back here IMMEDIATELY!"

Auntie Sylvia glared at the phone and, with the most photogenic of tiny smirks on her lips, pressed the OFF button. She glanced up at me. "Wrong number," she said off-handedly.

"Don't you DARE hang up on me!" came the shriek from across the street.

"Perhaps I'd better pop back over there for a minute," I said uneasily, "and just see if she's okay."

Auntie Sylvia's chin lowered, and she frowned ever-so-slightly. It was a most careful frown, one which no doubt she'd practised over and over in front of a mirror, one which expressed her extreme displeasure but managed not to cause any dreaded frown-lines to form around her eyes... "If you must. I do need a few moments to make a phone call—my agent, you know. Very exciting possibilities about a remake of *The Last Days of Pompeii*...and I've told the director, of course, about my *ever*-so-talented little niece who would no doubt *adore* the opportunity to play Lavinia, the loyal slave girl who sacrifices *all* in her attempt to rescue her rich, beautiful *mistress*—played by *me*, of course...We shall see what they say... but before you dash over, Mina..." And she laid one narrow, pale, red-nailed hand over mine. Her chin lifted, her blackened eyelashes fluttered, and her glittering dark eyes focused on me as if my face were the lens of a camera. "It's *not* that I *expect* you to choose *my* name, you know!" she murmured in a low, sincere voice. "But I would *strongly* advise you not to choose *hers*! It would make a *most* unsuitable impression...and I've *no* doubt that she'll come up with some *pathetic* attempt to bribe you, something *feeble* like dedicating her next *dreary* little novel to you. But you stand strong! *Resist* her!"

"MINA!" came the screech from La Plume. All the waiters and the other customers at both cafés were staring in horrified delight. I heard cameras clicking. I felt myself going pink.

"And when you've stood up to her *machinations*, hurry back over here to *me* and we'll chat over our lunch." She suddenly snaked an arm around my waist and pulled me close so that the photographers could lean in from their perches and snap a dozen shots, then pushed me away and held up her phone in a most photogenic manner so that they could snap a dozen more. People eating lunch at the other tables took the opportunity to whip out their mobiles and snap a few mementoes of their own, and then immediately started phoning their friends to let them know that they were eating lunch today beside the great and glorious Sylvia Goldduste.

"Run along, now. Auntie has deals to make!" And her phone started chiming in a most musical manner, as did the phones of everyone lunching at L'Etoile:

(BURBLE)
DAHLING!
(GURBLE)
SWEETHEART!
ALLO? MAIS NON!
(JINGLE)
OH, MON CHER!
I'M SITTING HERE
SHE'S SITTING *THERE!*
(RINGLE)
YES, IT'S ME

YES, SHE IS! MAIS OUI!

YOU'LL NEVER GUESS

I'D NEVER LIE!

IT'S JUST THE BEST—

(GLOOP-GLOOP)

SHALL WE SAY

A WEEK TOMORROW?

MORE CHAMPAGNE!

LOBSTER SALAD!

MORE CHAMPAGNE!

NOW, MINA, DAHLING

ABOUT YOUR NAME…

I was already halfway across the street when I heard the one last whisper:

YOU COULD BE IN MY MOVIE

DRESSED IN DIAMONDS AND FURS!

OH, YOU NEEDN'T CHOOSE *MY* NAME,

JUST DON'T CHOOSE *HERS*…

Auntie Persimmon was already bawling.

"MINA! Where on EARTH have you BEEN! We've been WAITING! Your LOBSTER is on the TABLE!"

"I'm so sorry, Auntie Persimmon," I said, sitting down on the café chair and spreading a napkin across my lap. "I didn't mean to keep you and Mademoiselle Azulai from your lunch."

But Auntie Persimmon had turned away and was cooing at top volume to the photographer. "DO get a shot of my niece and me! Such a LOVELY table! Such a LOVELY setting! Agnès, get out of the frame," she snarled in an undertone to poor Miss Azulai, who dutifully scuttled to one side. Auntie Persimmon raised her champagne glass (instructing me to do the same with a glare and a nod) and then leaned across the table, smiling like some lady out of a 1950s toothpaste advertisement. "SMILE, Mina, SMILE! I may want to use this photo on the back cover of my next book, *The Milkmaid and the Major*. I'm THINKING of dedicating it to YOU, my DEAR!"

"That's very thoughtful of you, Auntie Persimmon, but Mama keeps your books in a locked bookcase in her bedroom, so I wouldn't actually be able to read it—"

Auntie Persimmon waved away such inconsequentialities with one be-ringed hand. "NEVER you mind! SOMEDAY, my dear Mina, SOMEDAY you'll be able to discover for yourself JUST how much your dear Auntie Persimmon CARES for you!"

And I swear that there was a glitter of a real tear in the corner of her eye. It was obvious that her twin sister wasn't the only actress in the family...

87

And then the phone rang. "GET that, Agnès! And if it's YOU-KNOW-WHO, tell her that Mina and I are QUITE BUSY at the moment!" She picked up her fork, delicately speared a piece of lobster, and placed it between her lips. "Ah! DIVINE!"

(BURBLE! GURBLE!)
ALLO?
(BUZZ—BUZZ)
WHO IS—?
MAIS OUI? MAIS NON!
SHE CANNOT COME TO THE TELEPHONE
(*SNARL! SCREECH! SHRIEK!*)
DÉSOLÉ, MADAME! MAY I SPEAK?
(*SHRIEK! SCREECH! GRRR...*)
I SHALL GIVE THE PHONE TO HER

And with a tiny frightened grimace, Mademoiselle Azulai timidly handed the gold-plated mobile to Auntie Persimmon, who, with a superior little smile, languidly set down her champagne glass and accepted it. "Persimmon JONES, here. Who is speaking?"

Auntie Sylvia's cat-like snarl of irritation needed no mobile phone to reach across the rue des Jumelles.

"I *require* the presence of my niece *immediately*. Tell her that her lunch is on the *table*."

"You must be MISTAKEN, my dear PRUDENCE. Mina is in the MIDDLE of her lunch ALREADY!"

Not true! I hadn't had time for a single bite. And the lobster salad did look good…

"Maybe I'd better just dash across the street for a minute, Auntie Persimmon—"

"Don't you DARE! Stay right THERE!"

"*Mistaken!*" Auntie Sylvia had risen from her chair and was standing on the kerb on the far side of the street, hands on her hips, fire in her eye and looking dangerously like a prowling tiger. "Not likely. You know *exactly* what I mean, you silly woman. And might I remind you, I have asked you and *asked* you never to call me 'Prudence' in public. Has *that* fact slipped your *tiny* little mind, too, you *has-been*?"

"HAS-BEEN? How DARE you? And WHOSE last film was referred to by the critics as, and MAY I quote, 'a self-indulgent piece of TEDIOUS melodrama…'" Auntie Persimmon had risen, too, and posed beside her chair, fluttering her eyelashes like a silent-film heroine.

"Oh, let's not talk about the *critics*, Persimmon, dear," purred Auntie Sylvia, taking two careful steps forward. On either side of the street, fingers started pointing and cameras started clicking. "Or one *might* be tempted to recall the eloquent gentleman who wrote only last month in *The Times* how 'In her latest tome, the *once*-popular Persimmon Jones manages to make even the most energetic of bodice-ripping as boring as warmed-over breakfast porridge.'"

Auntie Persimmon stepped into the roadway, one hand clutching at her long string of beads. "UNTRUE! He never—"

"I read it myself. The whole *world* read it, *dear.*"

"And the WHOLE WORLD watched you STUMBLE on the red CARPET last season at the CANNES Festival, didn't they? A bit too much champagne that evening, PRUDENCE?"

"Don't *call* me that, you hack!"

"Talentless! AND a drunk! I've said it all along!"

"You—you *scribbler*! Mina will *never* pick your name, so you might as well give up now and let her eat her lunch in *peace!*"

"You AMATEUR! Mina has FAR too much CLASS to pick the name of some half-forgotten STARLET."

"'Half-forgotten!' Why, you—"

My aunts were standing face to face in the middle of the rue des Jumelles. A man speeding along on a motor scooter skidded to a halt and started beeping his horn at them, but they were oblivious—to him, to me, to all the watching eyes. I backed away a few paces—then turned and walked away slowly down the street. People were staring, and all the mobile phones of all the patrons at all the café tables started to click and clang and chime…

(BURBLE)

DAHLING!

(JINGLE)

MON CHER!

WE'RE SITTING HERE

THEY'RE STANDING *THERE!*

NOSE TO NOSE!

SPITTING CATS!

YES, RIGHT HERE!

WHAT WAS THAT?

(RINGLE)

YES, IT'S ME

YES, THEY ARE!

YOU'LL NEVER GUESS

I'D NEVER LIE!

IT'S JUST THE BEST—

(GLOOP-GLOOP)

THEY'RE INSANE!

(BUZZ-BUZZ)

MORE CHAMPAGNE?

WHO IS—?

WHO WAS—?

CAN YOU BELIEVE IT?

MORE CHAMPAGNE!

"Perhaps you and I will take a little walk, eh?" said a soft voice at my ear. I looked up, startled. It was Mademoiselle Azulai, with a genuinely kind smile on her worried little face. "Somewhere a bit more peaceful?" She slipped her arm through mine, and we strolled steadily away from the growing tumult behind us. I heard glass breaking, and thought that perhaps the hee-hawing sound of a police siren was drawing nearer…

We bought ourselves baguette sandwiches from a nice lady at a tiny storefront around the corner on rue St-André. They were only ordinary tuna fish, not exotic and expensive lobster salad, but at least it didn't come with a side serving of screaming and yelling.

Then Mademoiselle Azulai—she told me to call her Agnès—and I took a long walk around the Ile de la Cité, where all the important buildings like Nôtre-Dame and the Sainte-Chapelle and the Palais de Justice are, and she bought us these incredibly delicious ice creams from a little shop on the Ile-St-Louis, a smaller island which nuzzles up against the bigger island like a calf against its mother, and she told me amusing stories about all the other times that Auntie Persimmon and Auntie Sylvia had gotten into fights in restaurants or at parties—"It does not happen every day, *ma petite,* or even every week, but it happens often enough."

"Then why do you stay working for her, Agnès? If that's not rude to ask."

"Not rude at all! A very sensible question." She was quiet for a moment, as she licked her ice cream thoughtfully. "Your Aunt Persimmon is a very talented woman—as, of course, is your Aunt Sylvia, though I am never permitted to say that. Two of a kind, they are… And I feel honoured to have a part, however small, in her successes."

"But she treats you like a doormat!" I burst out. "Oh, I am sorry, Agnès. It wasn't very nice of me to say that."

Agnès laughed—the most unladylike little snort! "But you *should* say that, Mina! It is true… but then, I feel, I am a very lucky doormat…I have an interesting job in a beautiful city, and your aunt pays me well enough so that I can send a little money home every month to my family in Morocco, and I get to meet famous and fascinating people, and sometimes—" and here she winked at me— "sometimes I even get to enjoy lobster salad for my luncheon!"

Late that afternoon, after stuffing me with tea and cakes at Mariage Frères, a wonderful exclusive little teashop, Agnès took me back to Auntie Persimmon's flat. "She will not even notice you are here, *chérie*, I promise you," she insisted when I hesitated at the entrance to the lovely little tree-lined square where she and Aunt Sylvia lived—on opposite sides, of course. "If she has not been detained by *les gendarmes*—and it has happened before—then she will be in her study, writing, writing, writing it all down. As has happened before. She writes some of her best chapters after big fights with her sister."

We tiptoed across the shiny parquet floor and into a tiny back bedroom, charmingly decorated with pale lilac-coloured walls and elegant white curtains with sprigs of violets printed on them. There were real violets in a glittering crystal vase on the dressing table.

"Oh, Agnès, what a lovely room!"

"It is, isn't it? Your aunt had it decorated especially for you, years ago. And she bought the flowers herself, the moment she knew you were coming."

My mouth must have dropped open. "She did? But—but why? Why a room—for me? We've never stayed with her when we've been in Paris. Mama and Daddy always said we had to be careful not to offend either Auntie Persimmon or Auntie Sylvia by choosing one or the other, so we've always stayed in hotels, never with them."

Agnès just shrugged—a very French sort of shrug, lifting one shoulder a millimeter and letting the tiniest of smiles flicker across her lips. It said a lot without saying anything.

"I think that she has always hoped that you would," she said softly. "And I happen to know that there is a very similar room across the way in your Aunt Sylvia's apartment. Decorated with pink roses, rather than violets, but..." She shrugged again. "I will leave you to rest now, *ma chérie.*" A quick peck on my forehead, and she'd vanished.

Well, that was weird. A bit uncomfortable-feeling. This room, these flowers... It was, however, a *very* comfortable mattress, and even though it was only just after six o'clock, it had been a rather long day...but before I could doze off, I had to write to Amber.

I'd found a postcard with an aerial view of the city on it for the kids back at Wallywood. I circled the tiny image of the Eiffel Tower, then wrote on the back:

"Dear Amber, Joseph, Zach, and everyone— I wish I'd met my aunts for lunch at the restaurant up here, because then I could have jumped off when things went bizarre! No, not really... but I really don't think I'll be choosing either 'Persimmon' or 'Sylvia' for my name, not unless I wanted to be the cause of open warfare on the streets of Paris. I'll explain later—or you might read about it in the gossip columns. With photos! Love, Mina."

Making a mental note to post it first thing in the morning, I brushed my teeth, slipped into the pyjamas that Agnès had set out for me, and slid under the coverlet. I think I was asleep before my head hit the pillow.

CHAPTER NINE

Agnès had *chocolat chaud*—hot chocolate, yum!—and a buttery croissant and jam waiting for me at seven-thirty the next morning. She offered to accompany me to the Gare du Nord, but she seemed relieved when I assured her that I could manage it on my own.

"*Bien*," she smiled, "for one never knows quite when Madame will awaken. Most days, ten o'clock or eleven or even twelve, if she has been writing late into the night, but if she wakes early with an idea, then…" She left the thought hanging, and I hurried through my breakfast, gave her a quick hug, and slipped out through the enormous doors of the flat.

As I did, I heard a sort of moan, like a weary humpback whale singing in a distant sea… "AGNÈS! I must have COFFEE! *IMMEDIATEMENT!*"

I skedaddled. (That's a word my dad likes to use. He learned it when he was working at a university in America before I was born. It means to hurry away really quickly.)

And walking quickly and quietly (not tiptoeing, though it sort of felt like that) past Auntie Sylvia's block of flats on the other side of the square, I swear that I heard an almost identical moan as a certain star of the silver screen called out for her first cup of coffee of the day…

I do like the Parisian Métro—it feels really different than the Tube in London. Brighter, shinier, busier, more

French, if that makes sense. And I love watching people and imagining their lives. Riding from the Place St-Michel to the Gare du Nord, I had the chance to spy on so many different types—elegantly dressed businessmen, even-more-elegantly dressed businesswomen, students in jeans, housewives in raincoats, children in school uniforms, all ages, all sorts—as they began their day yawning, planning, worrying, wondering. There were a number of tourists with overflowing suitcases. And a number of pickpockets—you can always tell who they are, something about the way their eyes flicker about—waiting to see if any of the tourists might get careless with their wallets. Not me! Mine was in an inside pocket, along with my train ticket back to London.

It's rather an odd experience, taking the Eurostar train between Paris and London. It's a *fast* train. I mean, *really* fast. I mean, you're moving so fast, you don't even really realise it unless you try to focus on something close like a tree or a house or a cow and suddenly—flick! You've zipped by it before you can blink. There are long stretches where the train-tracks run parallel to a multi-lane highway, and you realise that those cars and lorries that the train is passing so swiftly must be doing seventy or eighty miles per hour—pfft! Gone. Left in the dust. *Fast.*

And then there's the Chunnel. The tunnel under the English Channel, or 'la Manche," as the French prefer to call it, which means "the sleeve," which doesn't really make sense to me. I mean, it isn't shaped like a sleeve and it doesn't function like a sleeve, so why do they call it that?... Anyway, usually there comes a warning in French and English and Flemish (which they speak in parts of Belgium, where the Eurostar also goes), and then—blink!—you're in the dark for twenty minutes. Underground. *Deep* underground. Deep under*sea*! Very weird, somehow, to realise that above your head is only a very flimsy curve of concrete and then some chalky rock and then a whole lot of salt water... I had a teacher once who told me that there was a glass roof in the middle part of the Chunnel and if you watched close, paid attention and didn't miss it, you could get a glimpse of sharks and whales swimming overhead. Silly, I know, but he was so sincere about it that I believed him, and watched carefully every time I went through... Well, I was only seven at the time. You believe a lot of silly things when you're little.

It's also a bit weird, I have to say, being in two capital cities within such a short span of time. You're in the Gare du Nord, a huge glass-walled and glass-ceilinged cathedral of a train station, and then, two hours later, you're in St Pancras in London, another huge glass-walled and glass-ceilinged cathedral, big enough to dock a zeppelin, if you were careful. 9 AM, you're on the Paris Métro, and by twelve noon you're riding the London Underground: Hammersmith and City Line, westbound through some of the oldest subway tunnels in the entire world. That stretch was built when Queen Victoria was on the throne, and hadn't been on it all that long... Off the Tube at Wood Lane, a quick walk under the viaduct, and there it was: BBC Television Centre, all curved brown brick and shiny glass and hurrying people, where Uncle Constantinople was waiting for me.

The building is basically sort of circular, with square wings sticking off it and a round courtyard in the middle. There are dozens of television studios hidden away in various corners and corridors, and everywhere you look you see faces that you've seen on TV: ugly ones, glamourous ones, all of them famous. Even on a Saturday afternoon it was incredibly busy. I looked longingly at the people eating their lunch at the sunny café, under the gaze of this wonderful statue of Helios, the ancient Greek god of the sun, high up on his pillar... Ah, lunch! My stomach gurgled at the thought. There'd been a long, long line at the sandwich shop in St Pancras and I was so worried that I mightn't get here by one o'clock that I'd finally just bought some sweets and run for the Tube...Hungry!

But I was met by a very elegant lady, Miss Odimayo ("I'm the associate producer of your uncle's show, dear. You can call me Cleo. Everyone does!"), friendly but rather brisk, in a beautiful pastel blue suit ("Chanel, dear!) with a silk scarf ("Hermès, you know!") around her neck. She was clutching a clipboard and informed me (briskly) that we had *no time* for lunch and besides, there would be *plenty of food* in the studio. I almost had to trot to keep up with her as she tick-tick-ticked

99

across the courtyard on her impossibly high, spiky heels. "I haven't been here since I was five or six," I told her, panting, half out of breath. "My class came on a field trip once, to see a puppet show, I think."

"Sounds *most* educational," Cleo said pensively, waving her well-manicured hand to indicate the rows and rows of windows. "They're talking about selling the place, you know. This will probably all be apartment flats in a year or two."

Well, I hope they don't sell off old Helios, I thought to myself. Gods get grumpy about such things... "Um, where exactly are we going, Miss Cleo?"

"Studio 13, of course, where your uncle tapes all his shows. One of the largest studios in the Centre, and we need it for all the people who fancy being in the audience. Particularly today... Why do you ask?"

"Is there—um—is there a toilet on the way? I didn't, um, go on the train..."

Cleo made a tsk-ing noise with her tongue, and pointed to a ladies' room just beyond the reception desk. I made a beeline for it while she took care of getting me a visitor's badge.

I didn't actually need to use the toilet. But I had had this awful sinking feeling in the pit of my stomach when she mentioned the size of the studio audience... and I wanted to splash my face and brush my hair before meeting my uncle… just in case.

And I was glad I did.

In an anteroom, someone dabbed some powder on my nose. Someone else smeared pink across my cheekbones, then brushed at my eyelids with something sticky. Then Cleo held a door open and practically shoved me through it, and bright lights speared my eyes. A roar went up. Not from an audience—this was a one-person roar. And the only person I knew who could roar like that (aside from Great-Uncle Frederik, maybe) was Uncle Constantinople.

"MINA!"

And I was enveloped in a huge bear-hug, and swung off my feet. And people were clapping.

Now, I know that you've watched *Constantinople's Kitchen*. Everyone I *know* watches *Constantinople's Kitchen*! So you know what he's like. You know how he acts. Big! Almost *too* big. Larger-than-life, as they say… He's a big man, tall and broad-shouldered, taller than Daddy, and he's always joking about the "proper little chef's belly" he's packed on over the years. "Nobody trusts a skinny chef!" he'll declares at least one every week, and his studio audience will roar back their appreciation, hooting and whistling, as if he's said something really clever. He's got a great smile, sort of lopsided and silly, like a happy Labrador puppy. He wears these heavy black-framed eyeglasses, thick and dorky-looking, but there's nothing dorky about him, really. He is a really good cook, Mama says. And a real showman, Daddy always adds. He yells, he shouts, he laughs, he weeps, he adds more butter… and people love it. He sells *zillions* of his cookery books.

He swung me around to face the audience. The lights were so bright that I could barely make out any faces, but I could see that there were rows and rows of them, rows and rows and rows, and rows beyond that, climbing upwards and backwards into dim distances. "This is MINA!" he hollered. "My favourite niece! Just arrived from Paris!" And while the audience applauded he said to me, out of the corner of his mouth, "And how are my two dear sisters?"

"I'm not quite sure," I told him seriously. "I left before we knew if the police were going to press charges."

But Uncle Constantinople roared with laughter as if I'd made some huge joke, and spun me around again to face the overfilled ranks of seats. "My niece! I am so glad to have her here! And I'm sure YOU'RE all glad to see her, aren't you?" And the audience assured us that they were and started clapping all over again. Some technician pressed a button, and the ever-so-jolly *Constantinople's Kitchen* theme music began to play. Most of the audience sang along.

SLICE THE ONIONS!
MINCE THE PARSLEY!
CHOP THE GARLIC!

JOIN THE PARTY!

THERE'S ROOM FOR US ALL TO PITCH IN

IN CONSTANTINOPLE'S KITCHEN!

CASSOULET OR

CACCIATORE!

IRISH STEW OR

MINESTRONE!

ALL THE FOOD IS DELICIOUS AND RICH IN

CONSTANTIOPLE'S KITCHEN!

POUR THE WINE, DEAR!

SIP THE COFFEE!

APPLE PIE OR

HOMEMADE TOFFEE!

FOR A MEAL

THAT YOU'LL ALWAYS REMEMBER,

ANY NIGHT

FROM NEW YEAR'S TO DECEMBER,

FISH OR FOWL,

MEAT OR VEG, BOIL OR SIMMER,

HE WILL SHOW YOU

THE WAY TO COOK DINNER!

COME SATISFY THAT CULINARY ITCH IN

CONSTANTINOPLE'S KITCHEN!

Far too jolly for my taste. And I've always had a sneaking suspicion that my uncle wrote the words himself, because some of those rhymes were terrible! But the audience loved it. Or pretended to love it. But why? Why laugh and clap and sing along? This is stupid, I thought to myself. They'd never seen me before in my life. And I was pretty sure that Uncle Constantinople had never mentioned me on-air before! So why were these people clapping for me?

The answer was obvious: because the cameras were rolling. And people will do very silly things indeed if there's a chance they'll get to be on television…

"Well, now that our guest star has arrived, let's get started, shall we? This meal isn't going to cook itself!" That was another of his catch-phrases, one he used regularly—and the audience went wild, clapping and cheering.

"Now, Mina, let me explain just exactly what we're trying to accomplish here, all right?" And he winked at the camera.

"Please do, Uncle." I didn't trust that wink. Who would?

He put one big brawny arm around my shoulder. "Remember a couple of years back, when we celebrated your birthday in Tashkent?"

"Yes, Uncle," I said warily. I remembered perfectly well. We'd been living there for Daddy's work, and Uncle Constantinople had breezed through one week with a caravan-load of cameramen and producers and make-up people, filming one of his television specials, *Spices of the Silk Road.*

"Well, I thought that together, you and I, we'd recreate that wonderful birthday cake I baked for you that day! How about it, folks?" he called out to the audience. "We could call it Chocolate Gateau Deluxe *à la Mina*, Uzbek-Style!"

The audience whistled and applauded its appreciation.

I was slightly less enthusiastic—you see, I'd actually had to *eat* that chocolate monstrosity, and, as I remembered it, it featured quite a few odd-tasting Central-Asian spices, in addition to a handful of grated yellow carrots (a regional delicacy) and rather a large quantity of the very sour local yoghurt.

"...Now, we have one hour to bake something that's going to impress all of Great Britain, Mina! So...let's—get—started!" And Uncle Constantinople, jolly and jovial as ever, bounded over to his studio kitchen countertop and began discussing the benefits of various kinds of cocoa powder and grades of sugar and shapes of non-stick pans, all of which were available for purchase, incidentally, on his website or in the *Constantinople's Kitchen* shop located near Oxford Circus...

I stood there in a blind daze for a long, long minute. I certainly hope that the cameras weren't focused on me, because I must've looked like a particularly stupid zombie. Baking? Chocolate? Cake? *Me*? What in the world was Uncle Constantinople thinking?

That this would make me choose his name, of course.

Why would he think that? Why would he, for one single minute, believe that thrusting me unprepared in front of a vast television audience to "help" him recreate a birthday cake (which, to be honest, I'd rather have forgotten) would make me choose his name?

And what could I do about it? I was only eleven years old!

Well... I could walk out, as I'd done with Cousin Alexandra. I could endure, as I'd done with Cousin Antoine. I could try to stay calm and listen, as I'd done with Auntie Persimmon and Auntie Sylvia.

Or I could try to turn the tables a bit, as I'd done with Great-Uncle Frederik...

"Uncle Constantinople? I have an idea..."

"Yes, Mina? What is it?"

"Perhaps you and I could have—a little contest? If that's all right with you?"

Uncle Constantinople's grin went sort of fixed and glassy on his face. *This isn't in the script,* his eyes were saying.

Yes, but I don't know what the script even IS! I said silently back.

"What sort of contest, Mina?"

"Well...you bake your cake—" and I tried not to shudder involuntarily— "and I'll bake one of my own. And maybe we can ask some of these nice people in the audience to be the judges?"

I did know how to bake. Mama and I had always cooked together, everywhere we've lived, and she had shown me how to mix a batter, how to butter a pan and dust it with flour, what temperature to set the oven and how to test for doneness with a toothpick... and Mama had a secret recipe of her own, one she'd never shared with anyone but me, she'd said.

Uncle Constantinople's eyes gleamed behind his chunky glasses. He's one of those people who can never resist a contest, even when he's a world-famous chef and his opponent is an inexperienced eleven-year-old schoolgirl... "And what are the stakes, my dear? What prize does the winner walk away with?"

"Oh, I was thinking of—*naming rights*, Uncle." His eyes went very wide, and for the first time that day, I saw a genuine smile on his face. It wasn't a particularly *nice* smile, you understand, but it was genuine. Genuinely competitive, and a little bit mean. "For the *cake*, I mean, of course. Whoever wins gets to name the *cake*."

But Uncle Constantinople understood everything that I *wasn't* saying. "You're on, Mina! Oh, Carla! Michael! Get my niece an apron and a mixing bowl and whatever ingredients she needs! Now, let's get baking!"

Carla and Michael, two ridiculously perky young people with enormous smiles pasted onto their faces, wrapped me in an official "CK" apron which went around my waist almost twice. They brought me a bowl, a wooden spoon, a set of measuring cups, and whispered where to find the flour, the eggs, the butter, the cocoa...

So. Deep breath. And another deep breath! And under the glare of a hundred spotlights and three or four hundred pairs of eyes, I started to mix up a cake.

With some tiny portion of my mind I was listening to Uncle Constantinople going on and on (and on and on) as he always does about this herb and that spice, "a touch of mace, a hint of vanilla, a *soupçon* of cloves," but the larger part of me was hearing Mama's calm voice in my head: *"That's enough sugar, Mina. Now mix in the butter. A bit more cocoa..."* And I must have been rolling my eyes and making faces when Uncle Constantinople's voice boomed out one or another of his famous bits of advice ("No one ever died from too much cinnamon!") because I heard the children in the audience giggling at me—no, not *at* me, *with* me. And I know that all their eyes were upon me—and I assume that the cameras were on me, too—when I pulled from my pocket the extra-large fruit-and-nut chocolate bar that I'd bought at St Pancras station and had never had the chance to eat.

"What's that, Mina?" came Uncle Constantinople's voice, suddenly sharp, suddenly close and peering over my shoulder as I took a little wooden mallet and started banging the chocolate bar into fragments.

"Secret ingredient, Uncle," I said, smiling sweetly for the camera—I could tell that it was focused on me, because the little red light on top was on. "For that extra chocolate-y goodness."

"Well, really, Mina—rather a *common* sort of secret ingredient, wouldn't you say? Bunbunny Fruit and Nut Bar? Hardly the finest chocolate in the land! Couldn't you have brought some Valrhona back from Paris? Some Debauve and Gallais, perhaps? Or a slab of Poulain?"

I tipped the shattered chocolate bar into my mixing bowl, gave it a few quick stirs, smiled, and didn't say anything.

"Well—well—" he stuttered. Obviously he was accustomed to people answering him! "Well, the ovens are hot! Let the baking begin!" And as this was something he said every week, the audience roared its approval.

But the children in the audience, I noticed, weren't roaring at all. They were watching me very closely, and with something like greed, as I tipped the gooey mess in my mixing bowl into a well-buttered pan and slid it into the hot oven. They'd never heard of Valrhona or Poulain chocolate, but I'd've wagered that they'd spent a good deal of their pocket money on Bunbunny Bars, mainly because you got an awful lot of chocolate for your fifty-five pence…And the television ad was a famous one, with that ridiculous cartoon rabbit…

Most of the cameras switched off at that point, as Carla and Michael and a dozen other assistants, all in matching aprons monogrammed with "CK" in bold, swirling letters, passed in and out amongst the audience with trays of little sandwiches and hot finger-foods. It's one of the things that Uncle Constantinople is famous for, these half-time snacks, and one of the reasons that so many people make an effort to get tickets for the taping his shows. A few cameras stayed active and panned about, catching people's reactions as they tasted this week's exciting new hors-d'oeuvres. I snatched a handful of these strange little puffy biscuit-y things with some sort of smoked fish and soft cheese and herbs on them, gobbling them fast and looking around for more—it was the first thing I'd eaten since that croissant hours ago in Paris! Lovely… and I could have eaten a lot more of them!

Then the buzzers buzzed a warning, the cameras flared back into life, and the cakes came out of their ovens…

"Now, Mina, we've chosen six children, selected at random from our studio audience, to sample our cakes, and to record their judgments on these white cards. You lucky things, you! Never thought that when your parents got tickets to be on *Constantinople's Kitchen* that you'd be sharing the stage with the chef himself, eh? And his baking whiz of a niece, as well!"

Three boys and three girls, looking anywhere from scared to defiant, sat on stools behind a long counter. In front of each of them were two forks, two plates, and two slices of chocolate cake. Uncle Constantinople's slices of cake—I could tell from where I stood—were dark, moist, light and fragrant with exotic spices. Mine, on the other hand, looked crumbly and heavy and lumpy with bits of unmelted Bunbunny Bar. Oh, well...I'd tried!

Six forks to mouths. Six mouths chewing, and swallowing. A break for a glass of cold milk. And repeat...

Six sets of fingers scribbling on white cards.

Six white cards held up to the cameras.

The verdict on Uncle Constantinople's cake? "Weird-tasting." "Sort of dusty." "Strange spices, full of chewy bits." "Where's the chocolate?" "Gag me!" "Not like Mum's."

And on mine? "Yummy!" "Better than the one that big guy made." "I like the lumps." "My gran used to make cakes like this." "Really chocolatey!" "Can I have another slice?"

There was silence for a minute while Uncle Constantinople smiled. Well, not exactly a smile. More like a grimace.

Then the crowd went wild...well, all the kids in the crowd, anyway. "Can we have a taste? Can we taste?"

And they started stamping their feet and pounding their hands on the backs of the seats in front of them. "Tastes! Tastes! Tastes! Tastes!"

I don't quite recall being hustled out of the studio by Cleo. I do remember that Uncle Constantinople was roaring, and not exactly in a pleasant way, and somehow I found myself once again standing under the golden glittering statue of Helios, and suddenly there was a silver-haired old lady in a flowered dress and a neat strand of pearls smiling at me.

Great-Aunt Wilhemina had come to meet me. To rescue me! I threw my arms around her and gave her the most enormous hug. "Oh, Auntie Wilhemina, I am so glad to see you!"

She gave me one of her sweet, knowing grins. "Had enough of your famous uncle, have you?"

"And then some... I need to find a postbox, Auntie."

"There's one right over there, Mina."

"Dear Amber, Etc:

This time next year you could be living here at the BBC Television Centre! According to a nice lady named Cleo, anyway. Not sure I'd want to, particularly after today. Not sure if you were watching the show today, but if you were, you'll probably understand why it's not very likely that I'll be choosing the name 'Constantinople.' My, but chefs can get angry when things don't go their way, and when they start waving those big knives about, watch out!... Anyway, see you Monday!

Love, Mina."

CHAPTER TEN

"You didn't! He didn't! She'd *never*—! You couldn't!"

We were relaxing in Great-Aunt Wilhemina's neat, book-lined sitting room in her tiny flat, hidden away in the labyrinth of streets and alleyways just south of the British Museum, sipping milky tea and nibbling homemade biscuits, and she was laughing so much over my adventures that she kept spitting crumbs all over the tea tray, then covering her mouth with her napkin, her eyes glittering, her narrow, cardigan-draped shoulders shaking with merriment.

It was wonderful, making her laugh! I think I started exaggerating the incidents of the last week—well, maybe just a *tiny* bit—just so as to hear her girlish giggle. And I think she knew I was doing so. It showed in her clever blue eyes... but I didn't have to exaggerate *much*, that's for sure!

"Such adventures you've had, my plucky girl!"

I always have such a good time visiting with Great-Aunt Wilhemina. She may not be rich and famous like all my other relatives, but she's smart and funny and seems to know all the oddest corners of London; she's lead me through some the most curious little back streets to some of the most bizarre little museums—collections of old dolls, or historical weaponry, or Victorian medicines—where she's well-aware of the importance of tea-rooms and gift shops. Now, *that's* the proper sort of aunt to have!

She's sensitive, too. Maybe that's not the right word, though... perceptive, maybe? Insightful? She *understands*— maybe that's why she's one of my favourite people in the whole wide world. She has this great little needlepoint pillow on her sofa—I was snuggled up against it at that moment— which reads "If you can't say something nice about someone, come sit here by me!" She loves a good gossip, but I've never really heard her say anything unkind about anyone. She just laughs if you try to compliment her about it, and says that she's lived a long time and seen a lot of strange things and that *nothing* surprises her anymore... She says she's seen it all.

"Well, your Great-Uncle Frederik always did want to get his own way—he's been a bully since he was a little boy! That's why I'll have nothing to do with that branch of the family... And dear little Alexandra—such talent! But such a show-off. Her mother, my youngest sister, was exactly the same... Oh, my lord! It is quite unnerving to hear about Antoine risking your life that way! Silly boy—though I suppose he knows what he's doing. All these years of racing and never a crash. *Yet...* Yes, Mina, I *tried* to read one of dear Persimmon's novels just recently. *The Dance of the Seventeen Veils.* It had gotten *such* fine reviews from the sort of critics who review such things, and I thought it my family duty to buy a copy, and I *did* try to read it. But I fell asleep before I reached page ten, and the book has fallen down behind the bed somewhere and I've never bothered to fish it out... Sweet, sweet Sylvia! How long ago it seems—I introduced her to Michel Misenseine, the French film director, you know, many years ago, when she was just starting out and was staying with me for a few months while she found her feet, and one night he was visiting friends here in London and they all popped round for drinks and that, as they say, was that! Dear grateful girl, she still sends me tickets to all her premieres. I hardly ever go. So much trouble to get out and about these days... Oh, no, I *never* watch Constantinople's dreadful little show! Does anyone actually enjoy cooking that way? All that fuss and bother and those impossible-to-find ingredients which he claims are essential to culinary success!...

"And now you're here, Mina. Well! You must be exhausted."

"I am, rather, Auntie Wilhemina."

"And still a big decision to make, haven't you?"

"Yes. Yes, I do."

"And—?"

"And I still haven't decided, Auntie. My head's all in a muddle!"

"Well, I've always found that sleep is the best thing for settling a muddled head. Why don't you go have a bit of a lie-down, and I'll start dinner and call you in an hour or so."

I stood up and gave her a quick hug. She felt so thin and fragile under her clothes! Like I could break her in half if I hugged too hard—but Mama always said that the women on her side of the family were tough as tortoises, and that Great-Aunt Wilhemina might go on to live to be a hundred years old, or more… "I will, Auntie. Thanks."

"And take the rest of the plate of biscuits with you, dear. I baked them for you this morning, specially."

I stopped dead-still, the plate held carefully in both hands—it was from her set of antique Havilland, which I knew she only brought out for special occasions.

"Oh…" I said, but Great-Aunt Wilhemina was gathering up cups and saucers and napkins and didn't appear to have noticed.

"And there's a little present waiting for you on your pillow. I know you're a bit too old for dolls, Mina, dear, but I was working on my embroidery last week and somehow got to thinking about the Raggedy Ann stories I used to read to you when you were little, and before I knew it—well!"

"Oh. Thank you, Auntie. That's so sweet of you. I'm sure I'll—"

And I had to put down the plate abruptly so that I wouldn't drop it. It would never do, to drop a piece of Havilland! I had to turn my face away so that Great-Aunt Wilhemina wouldn't notice—

But she did notice. Gently, very gently and slowly, her two thin, blue-veined hands settled on my shoulders and turned me around. "Why are you crying, Mina?"

"It's—it's nothing…"

"It's *some*thing. What is it?"

I gulped. I could barely get it out. The list was too long. "Nothing. It's nothing! It's—a crown. A dance. A race. A—a lobster salad lunch! A dedication in a book I don't want to read! A bit part in some stupid movie I don't want to see! A recipe for a—a cake I never liked in the f-f-first place!"

"And?" Her voice was very soft.

I looked up at my great-aunt's soft, lined face, so close, so understanding. I didn't want to hurt her, but… "And biscuits. And a doll. A handmade doll! Oh, thank you, Auntie Wilhemina, but it's all… they're all…"

"All…?"

"Bribes! *Bribes!* Crowns and concerts and cakes— bribes! Yours aren't so big and grand as the others' because—" and to my shame and embarrassment I started blubbing— "b-b-because maybe you understand me best and m-m-maybe you don't have as much m-m-money as they all do, but they're still just b-b-bribes! Every single of one you wants me to choose your name, and—and I don't know what to do!" And I sat down hard on the ottoman and burst into tears, real body-wrenching, throat-gulping tears, the sort that *hurt*…

Great-Aunt Wilhemina just stepped away and let me weep myself out. Anyone else might have held me close or patted my hand and said, "There, there," but Great-Aunt Wilhemina just stepped away.

That was actually kind of nice, that she's stepped away. That she wasn't hovering. Wasn't clutching...

After a moment or two I noticed that she was humming, something low and slow and almost sad. After a moment or two more I realised that there were words woven through the humming...

NO ONE EVER WAKES AND RISES UP TO SAY
THAT TODAY WILL DEFINITELY BE THE DAY
WHEN I SHALL TELL A LIE OR STRIVE
TO HURT A FRIEND
WHEN I SHALL
    DO SOME WRONG
    DESTROY SOME WORK
    FROWN AT A CHILD
    INSIST THAT I GO FIRST
SO WHEN THE DAY COMES TO AN END
    I'LL FEEL WORSE.
    NO ONE WANTS TO FEEL WORSE...

AND EVEN GROWN-UPS MAKE MISTAKES
EVEN GROWN-UPS' HEARTS CAN BREAK

EVEN GROWN-UPS FEEL ALONE
　　AND SOMETIMES LONELY
EVEN GROWN-UPS
　　CAN'T ALWAYS SEE
　　WHAT PATH TO TAKE
　　WHICH ROADS MIGHT LEAD
　　TO BIG MISTAKES
EVEN GROWN-UPS THINK "IF ONLY…
　　MUSTN'T BREAK…"
　　NO ONE WANTS TO FEEL THE ACHE

IT'S THE SAME OLD SORRY SONG
IT FEELS SO RIGHT—IT GOES SO WRONG
AND NO ONE WANTS TO GET IT WRONG…

I sat there, feeling—I don't know, sort of limp. Like a glove with the hand taken out of it. Crying does that to me, sometimes.

Great-Aunt Wilhemina, slowly and calmly, sat down opposite me and took both my hands in both of hers. "We all got it wrong, didn't we?"

"Oh! I—I suppose so, Auntie. Everyone tried, but—"

"Yes, everyone tried. *But.* Thank you for that 'but,' Mina. Notice that 'but.' It's important that you remember that 'but.' It's also important that you remember the 'tried.' And the 'everyone.'" She stood up and crossed over to the window, gazing out quietly and solemnly at the gathering twilight over the London buildings. Not looking at me.

"Your Great-Uncle Frederik—oh, there were some real characters on your grandfather's side of the family. Dukes! Nobles! Aristocrats! I warned my sister against marrying him, but marry him she did. Those people. That family. Hiding away up their pocket handkerchief of a duchy…So rich. So powerful. Forgetting, I think, what it is like for people who *aren't* so rich and powerful. But it *was* a wonderful wedding— you have to give them that. All those crowns and tiaras! I remember your great-grandmother, Mina, your grandfather's mother. Great-Uncle Frederik's sister. She looked so beautiful that day. Your great-uncle must have remembered that, too, and he remembered her special girlhood coronet. Which he took out of his treasury especially for you. That was a nice thing to do, I think."

I swallowed. "Yes, I think so, too."

"And dear sweet silly Alexandra. A scatterbrain. A feather-head. But an *artiste*, and a fine one. She remembered that you used to love ballet. I think, perhaps, that she has forgotten how many years have passed since last you danced. That's the way she is. The way she thinks. Perhaps she's not really been part of your life recently, now, has she? Have you visited her lately? Has she visited you? But she did remember. She did try to do something nice for you."

"She did." Why was there a lump in my throat again? A different sort of lump. Harder to swallow around. Was I going to cry again?

"And Antoine—Antoine would love to have a child of his own whom he could teach about cars, to drive, to race. Did you know, Mina, that he had been married once?"

I glanced up, surprised. Great-Aunt Wilhemina was still gazing softly out the window, the blue light shadowy on her old face. "No, Auntie, I didn't. No one ever told me."

"No one would think to tell you, Mina. His wife—well, it was before you were born. Giselle. A lovely, lovely girl. It was tragic—an accident. Their car was hit by a runaway lorry—its brakes had failed and the driver couldn't stop. Giselle died immediately, and Antoine spent months in hospital. He was—shattered. Shattered! Inside, I mean. His soul. His spirit. Many people said that he would never race again. But he proved them wrong. Ever since that horrible day, he has driven himself, as it were, faster, faster, fearlessly, taking more and more risks, bigger risks. He forgets, I think, that not everyone is as enamoured of speed as he is. That such things do not help everyone to forget. But *you* can understand why he drives as he does, I think, can't you?"

"Yes, Auntie," I said slowly, remembering back to those last frantic moments before the official waved the flag. "Yes, I can, I think. It must have been Giselle's picture he kissed, then, just before the race began."

121

"It was. His guardian angel, he calls her…

"And your father and his brother and sisters—what a family! Pure ego, you'd think, like four loud-mouthed frogs trying to climb on top of each other to get to the top of the froggy pile. But then… You never knew your daddy's father, did you, Mina? Not a very nice man—and I don't say that lightly! He wanted his children to achieve, and achieve they did—tops in their fields, all of them big successes, your father included in that, too, Mina. His expertise is in demand all over the world. But their father never once said, 'Well done!' to them. Not once, not that I ever heard. He died a long time ago, but I think they're still yearning inside to hear him say it… Does that make sense to you, Mina?"

Her words were dropping like large, round, weighty, darkly shining stones, dropping into a pool of thinking and feeling somewhere in my head where I hadn't even noticed there was a pool to begin with… Dropping like stones, settling to the bottom, glimmering and beckoning just below the surface, just within my grasp, if I reached… "Yes, Auntie. I think it does."

"I don't mean all this family history to be a burden to you, Mina. A lot of girls your age would find it so. But you've always been a mature little thing—my plucky little girl!—and I wanted to try to help you to understand why your relatives behave the way they do… Can you forgive us for it?"

"Forgive?"

"For not being what you needed, wanted, hoped for?"

"*Forgive*?" And somehow I was up out of my seat and across the room and my face was buried in Great-Aunt Wilhemina's shoulder and I was crying again, scalding white-hot tears—of shame! "*Me* forgive *them*? They should be the ones to forgive *me*! You told me just now to remember the 'everyone'—well, *I'm* part of that 'everyone,' too! I was doing exactly the same thing to all of you that all of you were doing to me—thinking of me! Me first! Me! Mina! Me! Mina, *Mina*, MINA!"

I felt Great-Aunt Wilhemina's soft hand stroking my hair. "Well, most children do just exactly that, dear. The me-first thing, I mean. You expect it from a child, but some people never quite seem to get over it. Grown-ups ought to know better—but often they don't. They can't quite manage it. Even ones who want what's best for you. Who love you. Very much indeed."

IT'S THE SAME ETERNAL SONG
IT FEELS SO RIGHT—AND GOES SO WRONG
   BUT JUST REMEMBER
   NO ONE WANTS TO GET IT WRONG....

I could understand that. I could. No one wants to get anything wrong. And I had a very big decision which, somehow, I had to get right.

123

Great-Aunt Wilhemina's hand was still stroking my hair. "I have every confidence that you'll turn out to be one of those grown-ups who *does* know better. I honestly do. And now a little supper, and then bed, I think, Mina, dear. You must be eager to see your mother and father tomorrow."

"Oh, I am, Auntie. Could I telephone them tonight and let them know what train I'll be on?"

"Of course, dear. The phone's in the hallway. I'll be in the kitchen if you need me." And she disappeared through the doorway, still faintly smiling.

Great-Aunt Wilhemina's telephone appeared to be about as old as she was. It was heavy and black and plastic, and actually had this rotary dial thing in the middle, like you see in old movies! You have to stick your finger in and push it round. It hurts a little, and it takes for*ever*... But Daddy answered on the second ring, and after shouts for Mama to come to the phone and exclamations and questions and laughter and gasps (especially when they heard about Cousin Antoine and the business with the Grand Prix), I got down to the real business at hand.

"Daddy, about the meeting with Mrs Grimm on Monday morning—I need you to make a couple of phone calls..."

124

CHAPTER ELEVEN

"Mina! Mina! Over here!"

Amber's hand was waving wildly over her head, and she had a huge grin on her face—I could see the glitter of her tooth braces from clear across the schoolyard. The place was positively heaving with children, shouting and screaming and running about, enjoying the last few minutes of freedom before Mr Patel unlocked the doors—at eight-thirty sharp! Mrs Grimm's orders!—and the school day began.

"Hey, she's back, guys! Mina's back!" came Joseph's voice from somewhere over by the sports shed, and within a few moments I was surrounded by all the kids in Year 6, bouncing around me, smiling, laughing, tugging at my sleeves, calling out—

"We got your postcards, Mina! Miss Marquardt read them out loud."

"Yeah, and we had to study all the places you visited for geography!"

"Did you really race with your cousin in the Grand Prix?"

"We saw you on the telly! You were amazing, Mina!"

"I've never even *been* on a plane! Was it scary?"

"Guys, guys! Calm down!" Amber's big booming tone carried over the thirty other excited voices. "We've only got a couple of minutes before she has to face the Grimm!"

"Yeah!" yelled Zach, an inch from my ear. "And we've got news!"

"News?"

"Yeah! We've got it solved, Mina!"

"Got what solved, Zach?"

"Your *problem*, lame-brain! Your problem with your *name*!"

"Ben's the one who actually came up with it," Amber explained, and then, as Zach and Joseph started protesting, added quickly, "but we all helped!"

"Ben's really good with words, Mina," Joseph said proudly, pushing Ben, with his crooked Halloween-pumpkin grin, to the front of the group. "He wants to write rap music some day—"

"I already do!"

"—and he thinks that—well, you tell her, Ben. And hurry! It's almost time for the bell!"

Ben, still grinning, started to do these funny angular poses with his arms and legs, and the rest of the kids began to clap in rhythm—not too loudly, though! Everyone was keeping one eye on the big main doors…

YOUR NAME—IT SORT OF TICKLED US

BUT GRIMM THOUGHT IT RIDICULOUS

SHE WOULDN'T TAKE NO PILL OR SYRUP

SO YOU TRAVELLED ALL 'ROUND EUROPE

MEETING UNCLES, AUNTS AND COUSINS

BY THE HUNDRED AND THE DOZENS

BUT THEN WHILE YOU WERE AWAY

YEAR SIX TOOK NO TIME TO PLAY

WE WERE VERY HARD AT WORK

KEEPING GRIMM FROM GOING BERSERK

    WE'VE COME UP WITH A SOLUTION

    FOR YOUR NAME SO PROBLEMATICAL

    WHY GIVE IN TO CONFUSION

    WHEN THE ANSWER'S MATHEMATICAL?

My head was spinning. "*What* are you *talking* about, Ben?"

"Yeah, Ben, cut to the chase," warned Amber. "Mr Patel is going to ring that bell any minute…"

Ben abruptly dropped his ridiculous rapper pose and looked me in the eye. "It's like this, Mina," he said seriously. "The first day you were away, Monday, it was, wasn't it, guys? We were all standing around over by the sports shed trying to remember all seven of your names. It took us awhile to get them right! We kept arguing… But Abbie had some chalk in her pocket, and so we started writing them down on the tarmac and we kept arguing about what order they went in—and then I had a brainstorm!"

"Yeah, Ben," said Joseph, rolling his eyes, "you're so *incredibly* smart. Now, would you get on with it? Mina doesn't have much time!"

"Well, I thought—maybe it doesn't *matter* what order your names are in! So we started mixing them up, and then, of course, so many of them are so long that they take forever to write, so we just started using the first letters of each name, and—Abbie, do you still have that chalk in your pocket?"

"Yes," Abbie said warily. "But be careful with it. You know the rules about chalk in the play area... I don't want to get into trouble with Mrs Grimm. Or even with Mr Patel!"

"I'll be fast. Thanks! Now look, Mina—did you ever think about just making up a new name? One that uses all the first initials of your full names, but in a different order?"

I looked at skinny, funny-looking little Ben with something like wonder. Something like uncertainty, too. "No..." I said hesitatingly. "No, I never did. But—"

"It's too bad that there are only two vowels, of course, and that that they're both A's..." Ben was kneeling on the black playground surface and scrawling madly. "There! That's it! That's the name we came up with! Brilliant, huh?"

"S-P-A-C-F-A-W," I spelled out. "Spacfaw? You think I should call myself Spacfaw?"

Ben chewed his lip a bit guiltily. "Well, yeah, maybe, if it'll keep you out of trouble with the Grimm..."

Abbie's brother Andrew hurriedly added, "If you don't like it, you could always spell it backwards! It's nicer, backwards, *I* think."

"It is *not*," growled Ben.

"W-A-F-C-A-P-S," I spelled out. "Wafcaps? What kind of name is Wafcaps? That's worse that Spacfaw!"

Ben drew himself up to his full, not-very-tall height. "*You* try coming up with a better word, then! We messed around with the tiles from the Scrabble box in the board games cupboard for *hours…*!"

"It's not that I'm not grateful, Ben," I said quickly. "They're great names, really—really!—and I appreciate the effort, honest. But—but they're not right for me, and if I've learned anything from this last week, it's that I have to do what's right for *me*, as well as for my crazy relatives."

Out of the corner of my eye I saw the tall front doors open, and Mr Patel emerge, swinging a large handbell. Still chattering away like an apple orchard full of squabbling sparrows, the kids in Year 6 lined up next to the Year 5s.

"So what are you going to do, Mina?" Amber asked.

"No talking in line!" Mr Patel sputtered loudly from the steps.

No one paid him the slightest attention.

"Well, that depends, Amber."

"Depends? On what?"

"On whether or not my dad was able to—"

"Hey!" a little Year 3 boy shouted, pointing at the sky. "Look! There's a helicopter! I think it's going to land in the playing field!"

"What? Where?"

"And what's that thing over there?" squeaked Abbie suddenly, pointing towards the church spire in the village. "It look like—"

"I think it's a zeppelin," said Andrew wonderingly. "There's a picture of one in our history book."

"Psst!" came Joseph's frantic hiss of warning. "It's the Grimm!"

There was instant and utter silence on the playground. No one dared to turn his or her head, not even when the helicopter noise grew louder and louder or when someone started shouting down from the zeppelin—in German?—and dropped an anchor on a long rope.

Mrs Grimm efficiently elbowed Mr Patel to one side and paused a moment to smooth her hair in her usual way—one swift swipe over each ear. Adjusting her eyeglasses on her bony nose, she surveyed her domain—and in a moment, her glittering eyes had focused on me where I tried hard not to look as if I were cowering behind Amber.

"Mina Jones," came her voice like a crack of a small, self-satisfied whip. "Good. I will see you in my office immediately after assembly."

And she turned with a snap. Her spiky heels pick-pocked-pick-pocked along the linoleum of the corridor.

The pupils of Wallywood School began filing into their classrooms—in silence, of course. Because who knew if the Grimm were watching or not? Some of the kids really did believe in her miniature spy cameras... Amber gave my hand a quick squeeze as we reached our classroom door.

"Good luck!" she mouthed almost silently.

"Thanks!" I mouthed back. "There are all kinds of luck, and I still need all the luck that I can get!"

"Mina!" Joseph leaned over and whispered almost soundlessly as Miss Marquardt started to take morning registration. He was really brilliant at not getting caught out— any time the teacher started turning around, Joseph would be sitting up straight at his desk, mouth shut and obviously working hard. "Just as we were coming in, I noticed—there are three enormous black cars parked outside the school gates! And one purple one! With drivers in uniform! And an orange Lamborghini! Are you in some sort of trouble?"

I felt a bright spark of hope ignite inside me. Maybe things were going to be all right!

"Oh, I hope not, Joseph. And—I *think* not!"

CHAPTER TWELVE

"Well, Mina, I trust you've had a productive week?" Mrs Grimm said rather condescendingly, smirking at me over her steepled fingers. "Close the door, Clive," she snapped at Mr Patel.

Mr Patel grunted something under his breath as he wrestled the heavy oak door shut before sitting down beside me.

"Very much so, thank you, Mrs Grimm," I said politely, sitting on the edge of the hard wooden chair and smoothing my skirt. Had it really been only a week ago that I'd first sat there? What a whirlwind seven days it had been. Not that I felt tired, exactly, but I did feel—well, older. More experienced. Or wiser, maybe, Great-Aunt Wilhemina might have said.

"I believe that I asked for your parents to be present at this meeting?" asked Mrs Grimm, frowning over her glasses.

"I expect them any moment, ma'am. My father had to make some arrangements, you see, about his work and flight schedules and such…"

"I understand. Well, if you've been a sensible girl, I am sure that there will be no problem about starting without them." She slid open one of the desk drawers and pulled out a large manila folder and selected a pen from her collection of them in a mug beside her computer. "An official school form,

Mina. A fresh, clean copy, free of rubbings-out and crabbed little letters—and which I expect to remain in this condition! Now, *Miss Jones*, for the official record—what is your first name?"

I took a deep breath. Oh, how I wished that Mama and Daddy could have arrived by now! But... deep breath. And another. And another! "Wilhemina," I told her.

She wrote it down in large, bold letters, nodding with satisfaction. "Very sensible, Mina—and as I said before, we shall continue to call you 'Mina' for short, except on official forms like this one. There. *Thank* you. And would you like me to put down a second name? For the official record?" She held the pencil rather like I once saw the Wicked Queen in a panto hold her evil magic wand...

Deep breath! "Frederika—" I began.

"F-R-E-D—"

And in a gasping burst followed it with "Alexandra Antoinette Persimmon Sylvia Constantinople *JONES!*"

Mrs Grimm's pen dropped to the desktop. She glared *exactly* like the Wicked Queen had done in the panto when Snow White had declared that she was allergic to apples. "*What* did you say?"

Mr Patel just sat there, staring, his mouth agape.

I didn't answer. I didn't move a muscle. But whatever expression must have been on my face, Mrs Grimm sure as heck didn't like it.

"I think," she said, and her voice dripped with ice, "that we shall, after all, wait for your parents to arrive."

"Yes, ma'am," I murmured, casting down my eyes. I had become aware of a good deal of noise in the corridor, and then the door to the outer office was thrown open and I heard my father insisting loudly—Daddy! Who *never* raises his voice!—insisting that he see the headmistress *immediately*.

I leapt to my feet. "Please, ma'am, I think they're here now." I gave the doorknob a firm twist, and pulled the door open. "And if it's all right with you, ma'am, there are a few other people to whom I'd like to introduce you…"

And suddenly that holy of holies, that terror of terror chambers, the dreaded Head's Office, seemed a lot less frightening—and rather too small. Because with so many big adult bodies crowding in, and so many voices demanding to be heard… Mrs Grimm found herself backing up against her filing cabinets. Mr Patel almost had to stand on his chair in order to make room.

Up to me to take charge, I guess.

"Uncle Frederik, I would like to introduce you to Mrs Grimm, the headmistress of Wallywood School. Mrs Grimm, I have the honour of presenting you to my great-great-uncle, His Royal Highness Frederik Augustus Johann Felix Stanislav Constantine IV, Grand Duke of Haunau-Braunau." Whew! I'd actually remembered all Great-Uncle Frederik's names, and in the right order, too! And he has almost as many as I do!

Great-Uncle Frederik (who was wearing a really rather magnificent military uniform with a bright red sash studded with medals across his big barrel-shaped chest) clicked his heels together and bowed from the waist, then took Mrs Grimm's right hand and pressed it to his lips. "It is my honour to meet such a great and noble lady. My niece has told me so much about you!" Great-Uncle Frederik turned his head towards me a fraction and gave me a very unsubtle wink.

Mrs Grimm looked as if she were about to faint.

"And this is my cousin, Alexandra Irina Galenka Katarina Natasha Vladimirovna Lyps-Hyanova." Whew, again!

"I am indeed charmed to make your acquaintance, madame!" Okay, so there really wasn't room in Mrs Grimm's office for such an elaborately low and theatrical curtsey—her chin practically touched the floor!—but Cousin Alexandra managed it somehow, and even made it look effortless and graceful.

"And my cousin Antoine Aurélien César Christophe Marcellin Maximilien Xavier-Marie LaVitesse."

"*Enchanté, madame, monsieur,*" said Cousin Antoine with a crisp little nod of his handsome head. Now it was Mr Patel's turn to look faint—not only had someone actually noticed him, but—a Grand Prix champion!

135

"Mrs Grimm, I'm especially pleased to introduce my Aunt Persimmon to you. I know how much you enjoy her work."

"A PLEASURE!" crooned Auntie Persimmon loudly, batting her eyelashes and twirling her waist-length strand of pearls. "ALWAYS a pleasure to meet a genuine FAN! And I HOPE you won't think me too FORWARD if I present you with a copy of my LATEST novel—HOT off the presses, as they say! Not EVEN available in the shops yet! *The Last Diamond in the Jewellery Box*—destined for the best-seller list, they ASSURE me! And I've AUTOGRAPHED it JUST for YOU! With my FULL name: Persimmon Electra Rafaella Persephone Veronica Ambrosia JONES!"

Mrs Grimm had gone very, very pale. Her hands trembled as she took the book, as if she were handling a rare and precious object... She bit her lip. "I—I can't thank you enough, Miss Jones! I can't tell you what this means to me—"

"Then don't TRY, my dear, don't even TRY! It's enough for me to know that somewhere in the world I have but ONE faithful reader!"

"And *one* is probably about the *extent* of them, I'd say," Auntie Sylvia murmured, fortunately too low for Auntie Persimmon to hear. She stuck out her hand and grabbed Mr Patel's, shaking it briskly. "Sylvia Goldduste. *Sylvia* to my friends. We're all *friends* here, right? And no one would *think* of informing the paparazzi that Prudence Chrysothemis

136

Proserpina Brigitta Halcyon Sylvia Jones had decided to drop in at Wallywood School this morning, *would* they? Has anyone *thought* to open a bottle of *champagne*?"

"Bit early, I think, Prue—sorry! *Sylvia*," said Uncle Constantinople with his usual cheeky grin and a silly wave. He beamed at Mrs Grimm as if she were a television camera. "Hi, there! Constantinople Jones here—or, if you prefer the long version, Constantinople Cosimo Humphrey Zebulon Malachi Macavity Jones. Never use 'em—wouldn't fit on a television screen! Nice to meet you."

"And this," I said, drawing her out from where she stood eclipsed by all my other colourful, *loud* relatives, "this is my Great-Aunt Wilhemina Cassandra Marguerita Scheherazade Linnet Diana von Honig. Auntie, this is Mrs Grimm and Mr Patel."

Great-Aunt Wilhemina stood silent for just a moment, looking Mrs Grimm up and down, up and down... She seemed to be looking right inside her... Then she said, very sweetly indeed, "Thank you for taking such good care of our plucky little girl."

Mrs Grimm had the grace to look ever-so-slightly embarrassed. Mr Patel mumbled something about "Names... they've all got names..." but no one paid any attention to him.

I was peering over shoulders and behind broad backs. "And—uh, Daddy?"

"Just coming, Mina," came the deep reassuring voice from the outer office. "It's a bit of a crush. But we're all here." I could see them now, once I got around Great-Uncle Frederik's broad backside: Mama smiling confidently, Daddy giving me a thumbs-up—patiently waiting their turn to meet the no-longer-quite-so-terrifying Mrs Grimm.

Huh! Wait a minute! What was that? "No-longer-quite-so-terrifying?" When had I stopped being frightened of the headmistress?

"And these are my parents, Mrs Grimm. My father, Peter Graham Jean-Michel Jasper Ambrosius Jones, PhD, and my mother, Elisabeth Johanna Michaelina Maria Lavinia Zenobia von Honig Jones."

"Names! Names!" muttered poor Mr Patel.

"I think that we're just about all here now. So if you'd like to continue—?"

Mrs Grimm looked like she'd been hit between the eyes with a cricket bat. "Continue, Mina?"

"With the question at hand: my name... you see, Mrs Grimm, I've had a week to think long and hard about this... and—and I'm not giving up any part of my name. Not one little bit!"

Mrs Grimm gave this weird little shiver, and if she'd snapped unexpectedly out of a daydream. No longer the adoring fan, no longer the awed commoner meeting a duke—oh, no! The real Mrs Grimm was back! Back with a vengeance! She cleared her throat authoritatively. *She* was the headmistress, and *I*—

And I was Wilhemina Frederika Alexandra Antoinette Persimmon Sylvia Constantinople Jones, and I—well, I *interrupted* her. "Not one little *bit*, ma'am!" She gasped with the shock of being interrupted. "And this is why…

"I have to tell you something, ma'am —that I'm really, *really* glad that you made the decision that you did, and sent me out of school to talk to my aunts and uncles and cousins. Because I learned some things, ma'am, some very important things. Things that perhaps I ought to have known before, but…well…I didn't."

I met Great-Uncle Frederik's eyes and he smiled at me under his enormous mustache. "Like respect for tradition. Like remembering the importance of family ties. Family history."

I touched Cousin Alexandra on the elbow, and she turned to me with her great luminous eyes alight. "Like artistry. Like working hard to impress people who are *very hard* to impress."

Cousin Antoine raised an eyebrow as I smiled at him, and the corner of his eyebrow quirked up ever-so-slightly. "Like bravery. Real bravery. Not how most people use the word, either, but the kind you carry inside you. Because you *have* to. Or you can't go on living."

I looked at Auntie Persimmon and Auntie Sylvia, standing next to each other, silent for once and—miracle of miracles!—not squabbling. "Like respect for one's gifts, one's talents, and using them to make the world a more—uh, *interesting* place."

Then to Uncle Constantinople: "Like showmanship. Sometimes you've got to be just a little larger than life, or…" and I shrugged, then stood on my tiptoes and gave him a quick peck on the cheek. "I'm sorry that I messed up your television show," I whispered.

"It's all right, Mina," he whispered back. "The audience loved it—that's all that matters, really. The ratings were higher than one of my cheese soufflés!"

And lastly I put my elbow through Great-Aunt Wilhemina's, and turned back to face Mrs Grimm—who was looking mighty grim, I must say! All my fine words weren't reaching her. She just didn't get it. Maybe she *couldn't* get it. Maybe she just didn't have it in her to unbend enough. But if I'd learned anything this past week…

"And ma'am? I learned something else, something *really* important—that everyone really does try to do the best that they can. *Everyone tries*…so you and I, ma'am, we need to try to find a way to fill out that official form, because in this last week I discovered that I really *do* love all my aunts and uncles and cousins and I am not giving up any of my names. Not one little *bit*! Not one syllable! Not one letter!"

And I am not calling myself Spacfaw, I declared silently. *Or even Wafcaps!*

140

Oh, but Mrs Grimm was made of stern stuff, all right! Her nostrils flared. Her spine straightened. Her evil-magic-wand-of-a-pen once more waved through in the air, ready to blast us all with an undefeatable spell... "Mina! This morning has been most unusual—most pleasurable—really quite wonderful, in its way—but I am afraid that I cannot permit—" She was in her own territory, now, on firm ground. We were in headmistress-land, where wayward pupils like me counted for nothing, were no more than dust beneath her boots...

"Oh, but I think you will find that you *can* permit, my good woman," rasped a voice from behind Auntie Persimmon. "Shove over, will you, Persy? I can't see!"

I turned back to Mrs Grimm, who was in the middle of putting on one of her who-do-you-think-you-are faces. "Mrs Grimm, may I introduce my Aunt Helena. Helena Amphitrite Carlotta Edwina Marie-Louise Saxonbury, QC—that's Queen's Counsel, ma'am. '*One of Her Majesty's Counsel learned in the law,*' I think the definition says. And I asked her to come here today because—"

"Because of this so-called *official form* of yours!" Aunt Helena boomed. For such a small woman, she certainly has a powerful voice. Even without her black silk robe and that silly white wig which she has to wear in court, she cuts an impressive figure. "Let me see that..." And she snatched the manila folder off Mrs Grimm's desk. "Hmm... Hmm... Yes, I

141

see… yes… Official? Official? HAH!" And she snapped her fingers directly under the headteacher's nose.

Mrs Grimm had that cricket-bat-to-the-head expression on her face again. I felt sorry for her—honest, I did! Even if it's someone you don't particularly like, it's not a pleasant thing to see anyone looking so flabbergasted and frightened.

"'Official,' my *foot!*" Aunt Helena harrumphed. "Looks to me like a photocopy of a photocopy of a photocopy—and I spy three spelling mistakes and two grammatical errors. 'Official'—hah! Balderdash! Who wrote this piece of twaddle, anyway?"

"Well…" Mrs Grimm's voice came out in a breathless sort of squeak. "I believe that…I may have…some years ago, of course…a rough draft…"

"Well, then, you can jolly well rough-draft something else, my good woman. This bit of doggerel certainly couldn't pass muster before the most merciful judge and jury in the land."

Mrs Grimm started sputtering. "But—but—her names! So many names! Too many! It's just—just—unseemly!"

"'Unseemly?'" drawled a low, melodious voice from the vicinity of Uncle Constantinople's elbow. It belonged to the tall, elegantly slender fellow in a black suit with a stiff white clerical collar who'd been leaning against the wall. "What an *extraordinary* choice of word! 'Unseemly.' Well. Fancy that. When I christened her myself…"

"Mrs Grimm, may I introduce my Great-Uncle Lionel Olaf David Peter Augustine St James, the Archbishop of Wessex?"

Daddy always joked that there was a picture of Great-Uncle Lionel in the encyclopaedia to illustrate the word *charming*. He could make a bow and a handshake last for *days*. And now he oozed over Mrs Grimm like melted butter over popcorn.

"How do you *do*, my dear lady, how *do* you do? Most extraordinary, this matter of names. Extraordinary, really. As if a person could possibly have too many…"

"I've six of them, myself," boomed Great-Uncle Frederik. "And who knows? Maybe I've forgotten a few! Ha-ha-ha!" He looked around brightly as if expecting everyone to laugh along with him. Nobody did. Well, back in Haunau-Brauncau, everyone *would* have done…

"And, of course, her parents chose them carefully, *most* carefully, you understand, in order to honour both sides of the family. Honour, my dear, that's the word—so important. Really now, Mrs Grimm, I must ask you to consider that word, 'honour'—you can't really expect the girl to honour one relative over another, could you?"

And nine pairs of eyes—ten pairs with mine, eleven with Mr Patel's—fastened unwaveringly on Mrs Grimm's blanched, starting-to-panic face.

I could almost see the thoughts ticking over in her head, just from the way her eyelid twitched or her lips stretched thin or the manner in which she bit the inside of her cheek. She would be stern—no, she would be merciful—no, she would laugh it off—no, she would summon a policeman—and then...

It was like a slow, steady sunrise, brightening her eyes. It was like a fist unclenching. It was like someone who's been holding a deep breath for a long, long time suddenly exhaling. Mrs Grimm smiled. And it was a real smile, I could tell—*anyone* could tell!

"I've just had the most wonderful idea! It will solve everything! Why don't—why don't I simply write down 'Mina, Etc,' on my form? The rest will just be—understood! Now, wouldn't that be the *perfect* solution?" She beamed at all the people crowded into her office—even at Mr Patel, whom she generally ignored.

Well, now... I *could* have said it! I *thought* about saying it! I *could* have rubbed it in, and pointed out how I'd made that *very same* suggestion a week ago. I *could* have made her look like a silly, pretentious old fool in front of all these important visitors....

But that wouldn't have been a smart thing to do. And that wouldn't have been the *right* thing to do. I glanced at Great-Aunt Wilhemina, whose naughty blue eyes, meeting mine, were absolutely calm but whose mouth was twitching at one corner. And I knew what she'd do if she were in my place.

So I smiled at the headteacher. "What a brilliant idea, Mrs Grimm! Let's do that!"

There are all kinds of luck, as I'd said to Amber before. And I said it to her again, later that day, after my horde of wonderful, annoying, maddening relatives had signed autographs for just about every student at Wallywood and then driven and helicoptered and zeppelined away—and after Uncle Constantinople had whipped up an amazing impromptu lunch from hot dogs, canned tuna and chilli-flavoured beans—with all the students (and teachers!) waving and cheering. Me included. There are times when I really do realise that I am a lucky girl. The luckiest of lucky girls.

And plucky, too.

And that's fine with me. Just fine.

Printed in Great Britain
by Amazon

73247019R00090